FOOTPRINTS ON HER HEART

HOOPER ISLAND BOOK FIVE

TABITHA BOULDIN

ISBN: 978-1-951839-42-0

Celebrate Lit Publishing

304 S. Jones Blvd #754

Las Vegas, NV, 89107

http://www.celebratelitpublishing.com/

*H*is life had become something from a horror film, only without the blood and gore. Okay. Maybe he'd watched a few too many slasher movies.

Trent Raines slammed the tailgate closed and swiped a hand over his sweaty forehead. One hundred and three animals. Ninety-eight dogs and five cats. Two Dobermans, a Labrador—

"Trent?"

His attention snapped up from the red paint baking in the harsh Hooper Island sun and landed on the blonde making her way across the animal shelter's parking lot. "Kara? What are you doing here?" He'd called her...right? Told her not to come in today. He massaged his temple. Everything in the months after the hurricane swam in a fuzzy haze of clean up and rebuild.

Kara Parker's blue eyes widened, and she froze, halfway between him and her yellow bicycle parked against a leaning loblolly pine. Her hands clenched around the backpack strap perched across her right shoulder. "Mel called and asked me to stop by today. Something about you needing help."

Mel called Kara, and now his website designer and photographer planned on helping him ferry a hundred and three animals from the mainland back to Forever Pals? His head ached with an intensity that left him reeling. He had a number of employees willing to help with this mission of mercy, but the idea of Kara joining him hadn't crossed his mind. Even after working together for a year, he barely knew her.

"I'll go." Kara's lips turned down in a frown. Wind whipped across the empty lot, blowing her pink wraparound skirt against her black leggings. Attraction clinked against civility, magnetizing each other into words that tumbled from his lips.

"No, wait. I'm sorry." He raised one hand and pressed the other to the truck, letting the heat burn some sense into his fraying emotions. "You surprised me. I thought Mel was coming."

Kara strangled the strap, her shoulders lifting as she inhaled. Blonde strands danced around her face as they escaped the loose ponytail she always wore banded at the base of her neck. Uncertainty pinched her lips even tighter. "Something came up. Zeke's grandmother...I think." She gave a delicate shrug. "Honestly, she talked too fast for me to keep up. Except for the part where she said I should be here today to help you. That there were animals in need of a home."

Home. Trent cast a look around the fallen trees ripped up and tossed about like a child's toys during a tantrum by Hurricane Arley. The squat green building, his animal shelter, the only one on any of the Independence Islands, had escaped the majority of the hurricane's fury. But his animals? He hated to think about the trauma and fear they'd experienced. To add on another hundred animals? He had to be crazy. What choice did he have? He'd made a promise.

The fingers of his right hand traced the line of scars along his left arm, deep gouges and grooves that lay stark and repulsive against his tanned skin in the harsh sunlight. He didn't need to look to see them. The image never let itself drift far away.

"Are you okay? You look a little sick." Kara stepped closer.

Trent jerked, hands dropping to his sides where they spasmed into fists. "Fine. I'm fine." And he did not want to make this journey with Kara. She'd be too much of a distraction. His attraction to her already risked crossing the "Do not cross" line he'd drawn when he swore to make up for letting his desires get the best of him and ruin everything he'd ever had. "Thanks for coming to help, but I can manage on my own."

"You're going to ferry a hundred and three animals from the mainland to Hopper by yourself?"

Her incredulous expression and crossed arms raised his hackles. If he had them. Funny how he now understood the expression. "You think I can't?"

"I think you're a fool to try when I'm perfectly capable of lending a hand. But you know what, if you don't want my help, do it yourself." She turned again, muttering something that sounded like "masochistic idiot" under her breath. "Good luck driving a truck full of animals and your pick-up at the same time."

"Fine." Trent threw his hands into the air, then laced them on his head, over the ball cap that would keep the autumn sun from frying his eyeballs. "You can come." *This is a test, isn't it, God? You're testing my commitment to my promise.*

"Oh, you're going to *allow* me to accompany you."

Trent grimaced. He'd poked the bear this time. Normally quiet and demure, to the point he wondered if Kara even had a personality. This version stalked toward him with all the poise and fury of a woman who'd rather slap him than help him. He deserved that. She'd done nothing to earn his rancor. And apparently, this kitten had claws.

"Will you please come with me?" Politely spoken, the words scratched an itch, a desire to let someone help. A feeling he didn't recognize until too late.

At his quiet tone, Kara halted. Her head tilted, reminding him of a beagle pup questioning the sudden change and searching for an answer out of reach. She would ask questions now. Demand to know why he'd changed his mind. Want to know why he floundered through this conversation like a puppy learning to run and tumbling over its own feet.

"Okay."

Before he could process the single word, Kara had opened the passenger truck door and slid onto the seat after dropping her backpack to the floorboard. Trent shook his head, attempting to clear out the buzzing sound left behind in the ringing silence. *Just like that?*

He moved toward the driver's side door, feeling ages beyond his thirty years. "You have everything you need?" He motioned toward her khaki-colored canvas backpack while slamming the door.

Kara nodded and scraped her hair away from her face, tucking it back into the band, where he knew it would only stay a matter of minutes before returning to flutter around her face. "I don't need much." She spoke with certainty but twisted her fingers together in her lap before shoving her hands under her thighs.

"Road trip rule number one." He cranked the engine while fiddling with the radio knob until heavy bass throbbed against his backbone. "Driver controls the radio."

Eyes closed and head leaned against the seat rest, Kara smiled. "Road trip rule number two. Passenger decides when to stop for food."

Trent laughed, the sound dry and rusty from disuse. "Deal." Holding out one hand while the other steered them out of the parking lot, he gripped Kara's smaller hand and tried to ignore the way her delicate fingers felt against his calloused palm.

Road trip with a woman he knew only through work to bring back animals from a place he'd avoided for ten years. This had the makings of an epic disaster. Ignoring the plan to relocate animals from the mainland was easy in the aftermath of a hurricane and a deadline that seemed far into the future. Now that the time loomed ahead, his palms grew slick on the steering wheel.

"I'm hungry."

Kara's voice drew him back from the winding trail his thoughts wanted to travel. Hungry...already? His own stomach grumbled and pinched. "Yeah, food would be good." No sense trying to argue when the gurgles told the truth. He hooked a left onto Palmetto Drive, pointing them away from the ferry's landing point.

"Um, Trent, where are we going?"

"We don't have time to drive over to Merriweather. Granny's won't be open anyway. We have enough time to swing by my house and grab snacks. Real food once we reach the mainland." Rolling the window down, he rested his arm on the sill and tapped restless fingers in time with the beat pulsing from the radio.

One hundred and three animals.

One hundred and three chances to repay his debt.

Broken trees lined the narrow road, their branches reaching toward Trent's truck. So much devastation and destruction for their small islands. It could have been much worse. Trees would regrow. Lives lost were irreplaceable.

Taking another left onto Summerville Road, Trent let the steady rumble of engine and music lull the initial panic into something manageable before taking one last left turn and pulling into his sandy drive, sending the truck pitching side to side and Kara's hands out to steady herself as a particularly nasty bump threatened to knock her head against the window.

Kara sucked in a breath when his little bungalow came into view.

Compact to the point of being ridiculous, what did she think of his tiny home? He killed the engine and glanced at his unexpected companion. "Home sweet home. Come on." He slid from the truck, hesitating over the desire to rush around and open her door.

"Women are like rubies, Trent. They are precious and should be treated as rare jewels." His father's words, spoken countless times, settled hard and cold against Trent's heart. How many times had he been handed snippets of wisdom, only to cast them aside as worthless and without measure? How often had his dad sat by his wife's bedside, watching her waste away, wretched pain contorting her? Through it all, his dad never wavered. Never gave up on God, while the pain of it all settled in Trent's heart, cold and heavy as an anvil.

God, I've so much to make up for.

2

*K*ara had enough time to bump the door closed with her hip before Trent rounded the hood and offered a rare smile. Her pulse skittered a tune she'd come to expect with him around. The seriousness in his eyes spoke volumes her heart answered without encouragement.

"Should I have opened your door for you?" He took off the cap, blinking sleepily in the morning sun, and ran one hand over his choppy black hair. "I'm never certain if opening a woman's door is cliché or expected."

The boyish charm and uncertainty worked something in her stomach, creating a flush that crept into her cheeks, causing them to burn. "I can't speak for all women, but I've always thought the gesture charming."

He smiled again, and the sunlight glinted off the dark whiskers covering his cheeks. In the past year, she'd never seen Trent as casual, albeit tense, as this morning. Normal Trent wore work pants, a polo with a Forever Pals logo slapped across the back, a clean-shaven face, and hair slicked into place.

One look at the scruffy face, khaki cargo shorts, and threadbare t-shirt sent a sharp desire barreling straight into her heart. She ached to wipe away the lines around his eyes.

Her stomach rumbled, and she opened her mouth to say... something. Uncertain what words might fall prey to her errant thoughts, Kara snapped her mouth closed and turned to face Trent's home.

The lack of flair, or anything really, stole her thoughts. Without the carefully tended lawn and fresh paint, the bungalow might have been thought abandoned. Nothing personal peeked from the windows or adorned the tiny yard.

Sudden yips and yowls came from the corner of the cottage where a pair of husky pups raced toward her. They barreled forward, all bumbling, oversized feet and open mouths.

Trent slapped the cap back on his head and stepped between her and the rambunctious canines. "Remus! Romulus! Stay!" The sharp demands set the pups on their haunches even as their tails whacked the ground and sent up a flurry of sand.

Panting, the matching pair whined.

Roman mythology...and Trent? The two went together as well as sand in a camera. Questions stampeded, sticking in the back of her throat where they would stay, preferably forever.

"Sorry." Trent looked over his shoulder, his blue eyes brighter but still burdened. "They're supposed to be locked up in a pen around back, but they're too smart for their own good. They escaped last week and tracked me all the way to church."

Bodies wriggling in delightful fury, the pups slithered on their bellies, inching closer to Trent. Their rusty red on white coats resembled a typical husky.

Trent pointed. "Remus is the one with a blue eye on the right, brown on the left. Romulus the opposite. Brown on the right and blue on the left."

"You named them after the Roman myth?"

"Not my finest moment in naming history, considering the myth says Remus killed his brother, but seeing as they're practi-

8

Turning the corner, she staggered to a halt, her mouth falling open. The yard spread out at least a half-acre, most of the space consisted of the best athletic obstacle courses she'd ever set eyes on. Tunnels. See-saws. Rope bridges. Set aside in their own fenced-off area, the course rivaled the one at Forever Pals. For all Trent's frugal living inside the house, he lavished the yard with bright colors and expensive equipment.

Remus chased Romulus across the yard, tail low to the ground as they raced with abandon. Romulus slid to a halt at the gate barring him from the bright obstacles, looked back at Kara, and whined while lifting one paw to the metal fence.

"Oh no. I'm not going in there." Kara backed away, retreating to the gate where she slipped out and turned, only to slam nose-first into Trent's chest. Eyes stinging from the impact, she took a step back and poked the back of her head with the metal fence. Assaulted on both fronts, she froze.

Trent reached out. Would he touch her cheek or perform some other romantic gesture that always had women swooning in the romance novels? His hand hovered, inches from her face, for mere seconds before he pulled it back and shoved both hands into his pockets. "Your hair's stuck in the fence." Turning, he tossed over his shoulder, "Snacks are packed. We should head out."

Breath tight in her chest, Kara detangled herself from the fence, leaving behind a hank of blonde hair. Jogging to catch up with Trent, she shook out her quivering hands. Once again, her fantasies ran away with her, putting thoughts and dreams where they had no place.

A man like Trent would never see a woman like her as anything other than a sister. He was her boss. Two strikes. Her earlier attitude made it three. *You're out of the game.* Kara gave a mental shake and pushed down the emotions trying to escape her control.

"Look out."

Her head jerked up in time for Trent's arm to thrust her aside before she could plow into the door he held open. Instead of cracking her skull on the truck door, her shoulder slammed into the frame with a *clang*. "Oww." Massaging the offended muscle, she tried to smile, only to feel the edges tremble. "I'm not usually a klutz."

From the amusement in his eyes, he didn't believe her. Then again, when did anyone listen to what she had to say? Sucking up a measure of composure, Kara pulled herself into the truck and closed her eyes.

One hour down. A million more to go.

3

lease don't be late.

Trent rolled his shoulders and willed the road to shorten itself. He sent a furtive glance at Kara, but she remained in the same spot she'd adopted after nearly clobbering herself with the door. Eyes closed, slender throat exposed, and a hummingbird-like pulse fluttering in the soft hollow. That couldn't be healthy. Surely such a minor incident hadn't caused this much embarrassment.

He'd found her clumsiness a bit endearing, actually. After spending hours together and never learning anything other than she had a degree in photography and another in web design, the sudden influx of information begged for attention.

Attention that he needed to spend on his mission. *No time for romance, Trent. Focus on the job. You have to fix this.*

He breathed a silent sigh when the truck rolled up to the ferry dock the same moment a long horn blew announcing the ferry's arrival. Not yet crowded with the Mimosa influx of customers, the ferry's deck remained relatively clear.

Presenting his ticket, Trent waved at the familiar woman and drove onto the ferry with only a slight bump to tell him they'd crossed from solid sand to shifting ground. An oxymoron if ever there was one.

Kara snatched her backpack from the floorboard and reached for the door. Without a word, she slipped out and ducked to the rail.

Trent grunted and removed himself from the truck. An hour-long ferry ride stretched before them, as winding and conspicuous as Dorothy's yellow brick road. But not as treacherous, thank goodness.

Massaging the back of his neck, Trent tried to duck around a small family. The youngest, a girl barely three from the look of her still-a-baby-but-toddlerish face, tripped over her own feet and pitched face-first into his legs. "Whoa now." He remained still, giving her a chance to regain her precarious balance.

She grinned up at him, her brown eyes brilliant in the sunlight, and Trent found himself returning the smile.

Stammering an apology, the man—presumably her father—scooped the girl into his arms and strode away. Trent followed them with his gaze, wiggling his fingers when the little girl threw up both hands and bobbed them up and down.

"Well, this is a surprise."

Trent turned, facing the familiar voice to find an even more familiar face. "Nigel! What are you doing here?" When his friend flushed redder than a cooked crab and shuffled his feet, Trent grinned and clapped a hand to Nigel's shoulder. "You're marrying Darcy."

"It's not official yet."

"Come on. You've loved Darcy forever. Now that she's admitted she feels the same way, it's high time you two make it official. Zeke and Mel are getting married any day now. After you and Darcy, I'll be all alone in my bachelorhood." His stomach clenched at the thought of being alone forever. Not his best idea. Then again, he didn't have the best track record in decision making. Not that he didn't want to get married. He did...but there were a few things he needed to do first.

Nigel cleared his throat, a lightness lowering his shoulders. "Where you running off to?"

Nigel's question sent Trent's thoughts careening back ten years, to the time when running away had felt like the only option. He shook off the memories.

"Overcrowding in one of the downtown shelters. They called a few months ago and asked me to help. The cleanup from Arley has progressed far enough that they'll be safe at the animal shelter." *Please, God, let this go smoothly. Don't let it be another disappointment. Don't let* me *be a disappointment.*

There'd been enough of those through the years. The pain cloaking his dad's expression being the most prevalent. People expected pastor's kids to be role models. Model citizens. He traced the scars on his arm again, remembering.

Nigel snapped Trent back to the present with a nudge. "Is that Kara?"

He couldn't explain the sudden flicker of tension bunching beneath his shoulders or the tightness in his throat when he turned to look at her. "Yep." She stood at the rail, camera raised to her eye, braced against the wind. Her ponytail gave up, freeing itself from the confines and flying into the breeze.

"...doing here?"

"She's helping me." Trent guessed at Nigel's words, shrugging when his friend lifted one eyebrow. "Mel's busy. She sent Kara."

"Looks like your bachelorhood isn't something you'll have to be worried about for long." Nigel looked from Trent to Kara and back again while a smile stretched deep wrinkles around his eyes. "You're sinking faster than a cannon-riddled ship."

"You worry about your own relationships. Leave me out of it."

"Not me you have to worry about." Nigel ambled away, his

stride easy on the rolling ferry after years riding the waves aboard the pirate tour boats owned by Darcy's father.

Puffing his cheeks with a breath, Trent blew long and hard, forcing the tension out. Spending time on the ferry with Kara. Simple enough. On a ferry this massive, they didn't even have to see each other. So why was he walking her way? And why did the smile tugging the corners of her lips as she stared through the viewfinder pull on his stomach like violin strings?

Standing behind her, Trent gripped the rail and leaned forward, attempting to see what held Kara in thrall. Playing in the waves at the ferry's bow, a pod of dolphins leaped from the ocean.

Kara pressed the shutter button again and again, the whirring *click* lost to the roar of waves and engines but so ingrained in Trent's mind after their days together at work that he heard it anyway.

"Quite the playful bunch, aren't they?"

Kara startled so hard she released the camera, sending it slamming against the metal railing with a crunch that rolled Trent's stomach.

"Nooo!" Kara lunged, trying to snag the camera from the air, only to nearly send herself toppling off the ferry and into the water. Without even a wave goodbye, the camera slipped into the ocean.

Trent snagged her around the waist, hauling her up and against his chest, where her thundering heartbeat matched his own. "Oh, Kara, I'm sorry. I'll get you a new one."

Hands covering her face, sobs shook her entire body. "It won't matter."

"I'll get you a better one."

"No." Kara turned away, pulling from his grasp and leaving him bereft.

Another day, another disappointment. Trent swiped his

hands over his face. If only he could wipe the board clean as easily as he scrubbed the emotions from his expression.

"I should have been using the neck strap. I know better." Arms crossed, face blotchy from wind, cold, and tears, Kara's resolute firmness shattered his heart.

"I shouldn't have startled you." He reached out, intending to offer consolation, condolences, anything that might clear the pain from her eyes.

She backed away, bumping into a man holding a corn dog in one hand and a drink in the other. Ferry food. The man grumbled. Whatever words he said leached the color from Kara's face and sent Trent rushing to her defense.

Her whispered apology was met with a dark scowl before Trent shoved himself between them. Eyeing Trent, the man shot a glance over to Kara, grumbled again, and tottered off.

"I'm going back to the truck." Kara marched, arms still crossed, body curled in as though to make herself as small as possible.

Trent followed.

Where Kara dodged around people, her slight frame slipping through narrow spaces and passing by without notice, Trent resorted to a more direct approach. Straight through. He called apologies but kept his stride even and controlled and ended up at the truck ahead of Kara.

He held the door open for her, enjoying the slight tilt of her head and the ghost of a smile playing with her lips. "You don't have to do this."

"If I told you I'm enjoying it, would you let me?"

"If I told you not to, would you listen?"

"Without fail."

Her shocked expression pained him. Had he presented himself as such an ogre? "I realize I've not made the best impression outside of work, but I'm not the type to railroad over someone else's wishes."

"What type are you?"

"The type you should stay away from." *Where'd that come from?* Trent closed the door and hurried around to the other side. Once inside, he threw his arm over the back of the seat, his fingers landing shy of her shoulder. "That came out wrong."

"I'd say." Kara eyed him from the side, her fingers clasping and unclasping around her upper arms until the skin turned white.

How did he make this better? Not only had he made himself sound like a pervert, but now Kara was trapped with him. *Make it right.*

Kara's head gave a jerk toward his arm. "How'd you get that scar?"

His hand dropped out of sight, falling against the door with a *thunk* that sent a jolt up his arm. "What scar?" *Smooth, Raines.*

"Forget it." Eyes closed, Kara plopped her head against the seat in a mimicry of her earlier posture.

With that single dismissal, Trent pinched the cracked leather seat between his thumb and forefinger and uttered words he'd never spoken aloud. Not even to his dad. "I used to handle dogs for a fighting ring."

One sentence, and his world spiraled down to a single point. He'd meant to ease Kara's mind, not make himself sound like the worst person on the Islands.

4

*K*ara stopped breathing. The reaction hit so strong she was incapable of halting it until her vision began to swim with a mixture of tears and oxygen deprivation.

Denial roared up, choking off anything else she might say. "No." The single word should have exploded from her mouth with the fury of a winter storm in Montana. Instead, it whispered as soft and smooth as cream in coffee.

Kara turned, facing Trent, her mouth opening to ask for more details. How? That would be a good place to start. How did a man like Trent get involved with dog fighting? He was sweet and endearing and not at all the cutthroat type she imagined a person would have to be to enter such a depraved sport.

Trent slid from the truck and closed the door with enough force to rock Kara sideways.

Her stomach rumbled again, reminding her she'd yet to eat. Digging through the cooler, she removed a pack of crackers and a bottle of water. Less than an hour into the trip and she had a silently stewing Trent. Yippee.

Why hadn't she told Mel no?

Because one doesn't say no to their boss' best friend when said best friend calls and asks for a favor.

I will next time. No way I'm doing this again.

The lie tasted sour on her tongue, killing her appetite.

To survive this trip, Kara saw two options. One, find Trent and force him to tell her every sordid secret so they could move past this kerfuffle. Two, pretend it never happened. She liked option two. Avoidance. A gift she'd mastered over the years.

You can't get hurt if you never let people see your heart.

Sighing, Kara replaced her snacks and glanced around the ferry. Here and there, people held odd food items with the occasional white Styrofoam cup that promised bliss in a sip. That magical brew that made all things right again when her world shifted out of focus.

And after losing her camera—and all the pictures of the pets they were trying to give a new home—to the bottom of the ocean, she needed more than the shot of espresso downed as she headed out her door at daylight. She *knew* better than to use the camera without the strap. *Idiot move.* The sound of Trent's voice hadn't startled her nearly as much as the quaking nervousness in her fingers when she'd realized how close he stood. Coffee wouldn't make the loss any less, and it certainly wouldn't help her jittery hands, but with nothing left to lose overboard, why not have a cup?

Twenty minutes later, warm cup in hand, Kara found a semi-empty stretch of railing to lean on while she enjoyed the sugary goodness swirling with pale chocolate tones. A drink to make her granny proud.

Trent meandered through the crowd, hands shoved into pockets and his head barely high enough to see who might cross his path. An image of dejection.

Kara sipped her molten goodness and pushed off from the rail, angling to intercept Trent. He plowed through the crowd, oblivious until her hand pushed against his shoulder.

"These hours will be miserable enough. Let's forget what's been said and done. Can we at least try to make the time go by without mourning every second?"

He blinked. Once. Twice. One corner of his mouth tilted. "There's a deck of cards in the truck. You up for a few games?"

"We talking Go Fish or poker? Cause I play a mean hand of Go Fish."

Trent's laugh eased the knots in Kara's stomach, letting her smile as Trent led the way back to the truck.

Hours later, Kara tossed her cards onto the truck seat with a long-suffering sigh. "You win. Again."

"Hardly call that winning. You're not even trying to beat me." Trent scooped up the cards and began shuffling with the ease of a casino dealer. Cards riffled through his fingers, the slap of plastic mixing with his chuckle.

No. She wasn't trying to win. Because the delight on his face, the way his body slowly relaxed with each hand played, was worth every loss.

The ferry horn blew, signaling their arrival at the mainland. Cards flew from Trent's hands, fluttering around the cab in bright arcs of red and white. "Finally." He left the cards and cranked the engine as another long blast sounded and the ferry bumped to a stop.

Kara kept the tension off her face and leaned forward slightly to see around the vehicle blocking her view.

Minutes later, they drove across the ferry and onto solid ground. Trent trundled along, his speed barely creeping over ten miles per hour until they reached a main road intersecting the ferry's traffic.

"You know where we're going?"

"Yes." Trent rolled his shoulders and frowned. "They took the animals to an emergency shelter a few miles from the ferry in anticipation of our pickup today. All the animals had thorough checkups and vet care. They've been in quarantine,

21

ensuring we can integrate them with the animals already at Forever Pals."

"Have you heard anything from them since they set up the location?" Her heart began throbbing, the beats coming faster as tension coiled at the base of her neck.

"They left me a message yesterday that I could pick them up. I've rented a truck, but I want to check on the animals first." He swung wide onto yet another road, leading them along the outskirts of the city.

"You have all the paperwork?"

"Should have asked me that before we left Hopper." When she sucked in a gasp, he grinned. "I have the papers. The rescue agency has copies. Regulations have changed, tightened, so there's less chance of pets with owners being adopted out. There shouldn't be an issue."

Like her lost pictures were not an issue. Kara pressed her fingers into the headache throbbing against her temple. What had she lost on the memory card? The last year of pictures from the shelter that she kept because she feared the backup files would become corrupted. Pictures from the hurricane, taken from her parents' house. Nothing irreplaceable. *Thank you, Lord.* The family photos taken at Valentine's Day were safe at home.

When they pulled into the parking lot of a derelict building more suited for sinister violence than rescue animals, Kara bit back the shiver dancing along her spine. Blue canopies dotted the expansive stretch of asphalt. Workers in fluorescent orange and yellow t-shirts with VOLUNTEER slapped across the back in bright white staved the panic to a dull roar. Buildings loomed overhead, cloaking them in shadows.

"It looks worse than it is." Trent muttered under his breath, leaving her uncertain if he meant those words for himself or her. "Stay here. I'll check in and come back for you."

Stay in the truck...alone? "I think I'd rather not." Reaching for the door before he could protest, Kara dropped to the pavement and immediately wished she'd worn something thicker than the wraparound skirt and short sleeve blousy top. Late fall on Hopper was a far cry from Georgia.

Trent held out a denim jacket, and she stammered out her thanks. Walking beside him while shoving her arms through the sleeves gave Kara an excuse to look around. The air filled with the barks and whines of dogs over revving car engines and the occasional scream of brakes.

"Marco!" Trent waved an arm over his head, and a black-haired man broke away from the group huddled beneath the largest tent.

Another man, this one larger and rather intimidating, with a buzz cut and beefy arms, lifted his lips in a mock kiss when Kara glanced his way. She shuddered at the bleak intensity radiating from the stranger and looked away.

Trent followed her gaze, his brows lowering into a squint before he reached out and clasped her hand. The gentle squeeze of his fingers sent a pulse of heat flaring through her.

Her random admirer gave Trent a scowl before he turned away.

The wind shifted, carrying the stench of animal feces smack into Kara's face. Her stomach revolted, and she barely suppressed the gag.

"Sorry about the smell." The man Trent called Marco pumped Trent's hand and gave Kara a cursory glance. "We're cleaning cages today and hauling off all the refuse, but in a place as tightly packed as this, there's only so much you can do."

Trent pinched his lips together but didn't argue.

Kara followed his example. Trent kept an immaculate animal shelter, but things here were different. These were volunteers, working under extreme circumstances, and she had no right to judge their operation. As long as the animals stayed healthy and were treated with care, doubting their methods served no purpose.

TABITHA BOULDIN

"Thank you for taking them in. It's not easy absorbing so many animals. You said they came from an animal hoarder situation?"

Marco inclined his head at Trent's compliment. "We do what we can. Now. I'm sure you're anxious to check on everyone, so follow me and we'll get the process underway."

Kara lagged behind the two men, listening with half an ear while they chatted about the rescue process, hurricanes, and sports. At that point, she tuned them out.

Marco rolled open the garage-style door and motioned them inside. The grating sound of metal on metal and the sudden flash of darkness mixed with bad lighting forced dots of light to appear in Kara's vision.

Here in the building, the sounds of a hundred dogs amplified and bounced until Marco had to shout to be heard.

Cages lined the perimeter of the warehouse, with the open space in the center a hub of activity. Marco led them that way, the word paperwork drifting by before the cacophony drowned him out.

5

*T*he next morning, as Trent drove across the ferry docking and onto Hopper—Kara following in his pickup—he rubbed the grit from his eyes and tried to see the bright side of his and Kara's adventure.

He'd learned something about his employee. An unexpected tenacity he'd never expected to see in the shy photographer gave him a punch of curiosity.

After the tedious hours of paperwork with Marco, they'd been too late to pick up the truck, much less load the dogs and make it back before the ferry closed for the night.

Kara had been the one to suggest they find a hotel—separate rooms, of course—and settle in until morning. With limited options on his small budget, he'd still bypassed several inexpensive possibilities when the tightening in his gut warned him that Kara's safety ranked higher than his wallet.

By the time he wheeled the large trailer into Forever Pals parking lot, Kara had parked his truck and waited at the hood. Once he stepped out of the truck, she came forward.

"Thanks for helping me." Hopper's familiar landscape, now

torn apart, set off an ache deep in his chest. "Bet these two days were more than you bargained for."

Kara shrugged. Her gaze locked on the foliage above his head, but her tired expression offered an open view to her fatigue. "Most things you expect to be easy end up sending you face first into a pile of poo."

"That's…an unpleasant image. True though."

Kara gave a heavy sigh while swinging the backpack. "You know, you missed a great marketing opportunity with the name of your shelter."

His brows scrunched. "How so?"

"Forever Pals is great, don't get me wrong. But why didn't you change the spelling, using f-u-r instead of f-o-r? Furever Pals has a better ring to it." She headed to the back of the trailer before he could respond, her stride long and purposeful as it carried her away.

The bark of tires cornering too fast brought her head around. Zeke's truck shot across the lot with Mel behind the wheel. Grinning, she bounced to the ground, wide eyed and full of adventure. His best friend since middle school, he knew that look stamped across her face spelled trouble. Most likely for him.

"Sorry I couldn't make it yesterday. Did you get them all?"

"We lost a few." Her head jerked in his direction, and he remembered Daphne's escape the previous year. "Not escaped. One of the transferred pups had Parvo. It spread through a few others before they could separate them." Although he had his suspicions about the loss of animals. Too convenient an explanation and no bodies left to examine.

And after seeing his old dog fighting colleague wearing a volunteer shirt while roaming through the tents…well, his suspicions flared. The look his old companion had given Kara raised Trent's temperature even now.

All it took was one man on the night shift willing to smuggle animals into the darkness after filing paperwork that the animal contracted some contagious disease. Marco squashed those thoughts when he produced official lab results and his personal promise that he'd managed the animals himself. Still...

Mel's hand on his arm pulled Trent back to Hopper's crisp breeze and the sounds of almost a hundred animals ready to be released. Tugging his sleeve, Mel pulled him around to the back of the truck. "How'd things go with Kara?"

"Fine. Why?" Trent busied himself with the padlock and cast a quick glance toward Kara but met only the open door of the animal shelter and the soft flicker of lights from the interior. She must have used her key to unlock the place. No doubt she'd already begun prepping cages.

Mel's huff, covered by the fakest cough he'd ever heard, reminded him of Nigel's remark on the ferry yesterday. "Did you set me up?"

"Noooo. Well. Not exactly. I really did have to help Miss Evelyn."

"But you could have called anyone. Why Kara?" Wrenching the door open, Trent stepped back to let the first flood of scent escape before hauling himself inside.

Mel grunted while following him. "She's nice. Pretty. And I never see her around the Islands. She might need a *friend*." Her emphasis on friend lingered several beats.

"So you sent her on an overnight trip...with me. I'm not sure what was going on in your head, but I don't like it. People will talk."

"You—"

"Hey, Trent, you got a minute?" The deep bass voice jerked Trent's shoulders back and snapped his head around. Lieutenant Christian Johnson stood at the back of the truck, his stance relaxed but with a certain amount of this-is-not-a-question in his posture.

"Officially or unofficially?"

"Let's say this is a friendly chat with the potential to escalate." Johnson rested his hands on the utility belt strapped around his waist. Not intimidation but a reminder that the uniform he wore meant a certain level of business.

Trent nodded to Mel. "You'll get started?"

"Yeah...sure." Mel gave Christian a quizzical glance before pulling the first dog's leash into her hand and moving to release the latch on his crate.

Jumping out of the truck, Trent landed lightly on the balls of his feet and jerked his head toward the opposite edge of the parking lot. Well out of Mel's and Kara's earshot. Whatever reason brought Mimosa's police to his door, neither woman needed to know.

"You got all the animals you went for?" Johnson's tone showed true curiosity and gratefulness, but Trent shrugged it away.

"We both know you're not here about the animals. What's up?"

"Your old pal's been spotted on Mimosa. Within hours of a string of lootings from some of the more exposed buildings. Guess he thought the Islands would be easy pickings after the hurricane."

After letting the implication dangle for more than a minute, Trent crossed his arms. "The only people I care anything about live right here on the Islands."

"You know that's not who I mean."

"Are you saying I need an alibi?" He locked gazes with Christian and infused truth into his voice. "I left that life behind years ago."

"Some things refuse to stay in the past, Trent. That old life, the easy money, it works on a man."

"Not this one. I'm done. Out. If I knew anything, you'd be the first person to know. But I don't. Now, if you don't mind, I need to get back to work."

"You got your second chance. Don't blow it."

"Didn't plan on it." Anger at being implicated in the break-ins rose, hot and furious, soothed only by the sight of his building shimmering in waves of heat. "I saw Snake on the mainland. Not intentionally. He's working as a volunteer at Marco's rescue. You might check into that."

Trent waited for the nod that said walking away wouldn't get him arrested before turning on his heel.

He avoided the curious looks and threw himself into the job at hand. With every animal leaving the truck, he made a promise to find them a happy, loving home. His debt needed repaying.

"Trent—"

"Don't, Mel." Holding up his hand as though to ward off a blow, Trent retreated one last time into the truck. The last dog, a schnauzer mix named Toby, hunkered in the back of his cage, legs trembling and a low growl rumbling from his throat. "Easy, big guy." Trent reached for the leash, and the dog pressed harder into the back of the cage.

"Poor fella." Mel lowered to her haunches and peered into the cage. "He needs a friend, too."

His thoughts snapped to Kara, who stood at the back of the truck, waiting.

Mel stood and patted his shoulder. "I'm headed home. I'll be back tomorrow to start grooming." She enveloped Kara in a hug after jumping down from the truck and disappeared into the shadows.

When had it become nighttime?

Massaging his eyes, he checked his watch and groaned. "Kara, I'm sorry. I didn't realize how late it was. You should go home."

"I heard what you told Christian."

Which part? He wanted to ask, but the answer showed in

Kara's crossed arms. She leaned from side to side, no doubt worn out from the long day and exertion.

"Does this have anything to do with what you told me on the ferry? Or that creepy guy at the rescue center?"

Right. He had mentioned his past life in a moment of utter recklessness. Mel believed he'd started the animal shelter because he loved the animals, but that reality only answered part of the story.

"If I ask you to trust me, will you? What happened back then, it doesn't matter now." Unless he considered daily penance to be something that mattered. A lot.

"Our past is more than something we can sweep under the rug and forget about because it's inconvenient. It haunts us— sometimes daily—of what we've done wrong. What we could have done better. People we've hurt." Her voice dropped to a whisper, and he leaned forward. "Things that have hurt us shaped us into who we are today."

With those words, Kara backed away, her soft-soled shoes barely sounding over his heart's pounding beat.

Trent let her retreat, her words hammering blows he longed to dodge but no longer had the strength to avoid. If what she said was true, then what kind of man was he today because of the actions he'd taken?

6

*D*elighted squeals from her nieces and nephews pulled Kara toward the water's edge. Ages four through fourteen, the group had made a game out of running from the waves. Savannah, the smallest, shrieked and ran toward her older sister, Lacey, who scooped the youngster up and ran them toward dry sand.

Savannah clapped chubby hands, shouting, "Again! Again!"

Dylan, Eric, and Logan, her oldest brother's three boys, admired a massive sandcastle bulging from the sand beyond the water's edge.

Her mother's voice carried from the large porch jutting out toward the pavilion where most of the family had gathered for the annual Parker family reunion. Four generations. A dozen grandchildren and great-grandchildren. Kara lost count of the total number of family members roaming Hopper's beach. Tomorrow, they would flood back to their own homes after packing Life Walk Church for the morning service.

Another shout, this one more intense than the first, called for everyone to gather and sent feet scurrying toward the house.

Kara followed, her steps slower than the others until she

became the last of the pack forming a line snaking around the tables overflowing with food.

"Aunt Kara!" Savannah wriggled from her mother's arms, her hands stretching toward Kara. "Down, Mama."

Kara dropped to a knee and wrapped her arms around the wriggling little girl, taking a deep breath of sweet sunshine and playful toddler.

"You need a few of those." Her brother Matthew scooped Savannah up and tweaked her nose.

"Back off, Matt." Kara folded her arms and scowled. With the whole family around, the last thing she wanted to discuss was her love life. Or lack thereof. "It's none of your business."

"I'm your brother. Everything is my business. Including the fact you took off to the mainland with your boss for two days. Not giving off the best impression there, sis." He shook his head, the smirk making her want to crawl into a hole and never emerge. "What would Grandma say?"

"She'd say 'Leave your sister alone and worry about your own self.'" Grandma Parker whacked Matt's knee with her cane before looping her arm around Kara's waist and giving her a squeeze. "Fix me a plate, dearie?"

Relief flooded through Kara. Saved by Grandma's cane.

"You bet." Kara kissed the wrinkled cheek and waited until Grandma settled herself on a nearby bench and engaged in conversation before she returned her attention to the people filling the bench seats.

Tight little knots of individual families became evident if you knew the relationships as she did. The overall chaos stayed controlled by the single loudest voice. Paulette Parker orchestrated the line with the skill of a drill sergeant. "Matthew, you fix a plate for Savannah while you're standing there. Delanie, your dog is about to take off with the ham. Put him around back with the others."

Kara moved through the line, heaping the two plates with all her favorites before retreating to the table where Grandma Parker waited. "Here you go, Granny." Sliding the plate within her reach, Kara lowered herself to the bench seat and took her first bite of her mother's signature slow-roasted chicken.

"Where's my dessert?" Granny Parker poked her fork through the mashed potatoes and harrumphed. "I'm too old to have to clean my plate before I get the good stuff. Kara, do me a favor and fix us a plate of goodies."

A bony elbow poked Kara's ribs, and she stifled a chuckle when Granny winked.

First to the dessert table, Kara had her choice of cakes, pies, cookies, and an assortment of dishes she had no way of identifying except by the luxurious smells of chocolate and peanut butter. Knowing Granny's proclivity for pie, Kara took a slice of apple and pecan before moving to the banana bread, pumpkin swirl bread, and a handful of white chocolate macadamia nut cookies.

"Kara!" Her mother stood across from her, hands on hips and a deep frown pulling her normally pretty face around until she appeared distraught. "Really, dessert first? What kind of example are you setting for the little ones if they see you over here eating sweets instead of decent food?"

"I think their parents can tell them that when they're adults they can eat dessert first too." Kara jutted her chin, heart thundering at the rebellion brewing in her veins. She hid her shaking hands behind the burnt-orange tablecloth. "It's not a big deal, Mom. Granny asked me to get her some dessert. You know how she is about her pie and cookies."

Dropping her arms, her mother huffed a breath. "Oh, all right. We're supposed to be having fun. I suppose dessert first isn't that big a deal. Don't tell the others."

Kara fumbled the plate, nearly dropping the food when her mother snatched a cookie from the ornamental platter and took an enormous bite.

Go figure. Her mother only backed off once Kara brought Granny into the mix. Drawing her scattered courage back together, Kara returned to Granny, who promptly devoured the apple pie and a cookie.

Kara poked through her food, no longer interested in satiating the empty pit her stomach had become. Her phone jingled, and she dove for the distraction. Trent's name popped up on the screen, sending Kara's pulse into a wild flurry. All their conversations from the ferry ride and after played on repeat. Trent never called. Which meant one thing. After thinking it over a few days, he'd decided he didn't want an employee who talked back. No doubt he'd fire her.

He said he'd listen, and he did. Did he regret it?

Her finger hovered over the button, a slight shake evident as her adrenaline spiked. Sliding her finger along the green button, she cleared her throat and squeaked out a hello.

"Sorry to bother you on the weekend, but I need your help." His footsteps trickled through the phone, boots on concrete. "Do you think you could spare a few hours later this afternoon?"

"Are the animals okay?"

"Oh, they're fine. I have an idea, and I need your input. Come by after closing? It'll be quiet then." As though to argue against Trent's remark, a series of barks drowned out his voice.

The flood of relief left her lightheaded. Kara scanned the family gathering, but no one paid any attention to her. Par for the course. "Sure. Give me a few hours." One thing they *would* notice is her disappearing before the annual round of games.

A chorus of squeals and toddler-sized shouts ricocheted from the small tables where all the kids below the age of ten sat with mouths gaping.

"...busy."

Kara pressed her finger into her free ear to cut off the noise.

Whatever had happened with the children, she'd let the parents deal with it. "Sorry, Trent. I missed that. Hold on."

"Are you talking to a *boy?*" Granny wiggled her eyebrows, nearly spitting out her false teeth with the force of her question.

"It's my boss, Granny." Kara hurried away before Granny spread the word.

"If I'm interrupting, I can call back later." Trent's hesitation endeared him to her heart when he ignored the shrill whistles of her brothers piercing through the air loud enough to break the sound barrier. A certain assurance Granny'd announced Kara's call.

"No. It's fine." The ocean beckoned, a sweet lullaby promising peace and rest. Kara paced out of reach of the rolling waves while continually scanning the crowd of family. Let them try to sneak close enough to hear the conversation. Family. Equal parts amazing and annoying. She loved them, no doubt, but every now and then she wouldn't mind burying them in sand, so they'd leave her alone. "What do you need me to help you with?"

"I want to have an adoption day. At Christmas. The shelter is full, and with everything that happened with the hurricane, I'm afraid it will get worse. I won't send them back to the mainland. We need families here." He ended on a hard note, and she imagined him pacing the aisle, eyes drawn to the sad faces lining either side while they waited for someone to save them.

"I'm not an event coordinator." Better to get that out in the open now than see the disappointment in his eyes later when she failed to measure up to his expectations.

"But you're organized, competent, and you write a killer byline for the website. I need you to do this for me. I'll pay whatever you ask."

Do this for me. The plea lodged itself in her heart, begging to be wrapped up like a Christmas present to be ogled at every chance. Kara rolled her eyes, since no one hovered around to see the display of youthful impatience. "You can pay me my normal wage."

"Plus a new camera since it's my fault yours took a dive." Static crackled through the connection thanks to the repairs still underway. Trent's voice popped, rising and falling so that all she heard was "...thanks...later" before the line went dead.

Grinning and hugging the phone to her chest, Kara spun in a circle before thinking better of it. The sight of her family hovering at the edge of the pavilion brought her back down to the sand with a rush.

"Your boss calls your private number on Saturdays?" Matthew grinned and mimicked her twirl. "I think little Kara has a crush."

"Grow up." Kara tossed her hair over her shoulder and glared. "He asked me to come help him. With an adoption campaign for Christmas."

"That's a wonderful idea." Her mother placed a palm on Dad's stomach when he opened his mouth.

After sending a quick glance at Kara, then at his wife, while rubbing a palm over his ribs, he nodded. "Sure. Sure. You're not leaving now, are you?"

"In a few hours. You know I can't miss the horseshoe tournament. I hold the record high score." Kara returned to her seat and forked up a bite of chicken, her appetite returning with a vengeance. Tangy sauce mixed with a melt-in-your-mouth tenderness that made her think of Trent. Gruff and edgy on the outside, but butter in the center. Oh, how he'd hate knowing she'd made that comparison. She stifled a chuckle, covering her mouth when Granny wiggled her eyebrows with a look that said she'd read Kara's mind.

7

*T*rent ended the call and spun the phone in his hand, ready to slide it into his pocket, when it buzzed with an unfamiliar number. He answered with a sigh, expecting to hear from another islander asking if he had room to board their pet while they remodeled.

"Long time, bro." The hiss of breath, the whistle of air pressing through gapped teeth doused Trent with a coldness he'd only experienced once before.

"Snake. How'd you get this number?"

"Marco's rather easy to manipulate, when you know the right questions to ask." A thud of iron striking iron clanged through the connection. "How's business?"

"None of yours." Trent ended the call, fumbling the phone into his pocket with shaking hands.

Should he call Deputy Johnson, tell him about the call? Risk the entire Mimosa police force crashing down on his island as they searched for a man who just as likely called from the mainland as from the house next door?

God, I don't know what to do.

His pocket rumbled, and the phone slipped into his hand.

Johnson's name and number slid across the screen. *I'll take that as a sign.* His "Hello" cut off as Christian cut in.

"There's been another break-in."

"I think I know who's behind it. One of the old gang called me." Trent scuffed his shoe across the concrete and grimaced. "I don't know where he is, but he found me."

"I'm headed your way. Don't go anywhere." Johnson hung up, the click of his receiver loud in Trent's ear.

Okay. Now what? Kara and Johnson were both on their way to the shelter, and unless he called and told Kara not to come, there'd be no keeping this from her.

What did it matter if she found out her boss' true nature? Clapping his hands over his neck, Trent squeezed. Who would he really be protecting if he kept Kara from learning the truth? The tendon running beneath his palms spasmed. *Why do you care so much if Kara knows? Would you act this way if it were Mel on her way here?*

"Hey, boss, I finished cleaning out the cages on the list. Dot's working on the food and water. You want me to start on the cats' cages?" John, one of Trent's high school workers, waited at the end of the corridor wearing yellow rubber gloves stretched over his forearms and a plastic poncho to protect his clothes.

"Sure." Trent nodded and released his hands. "I'll start exercising."

John nodded and backed away, his sneakers squeaking on the clean concrete floor.

Trent clapped his hands and retreated to the office where he grabbed a leash before heading back to the cages and calling for Hermes. The agile greyhound stood, his eyes wary and body alert but with no sign of aggression or fear. Upon seeing the leash, the long tail whacked each side of the cage.

"Let's run some laps."

Hours later, after running the obstacle course and a full perimeter circle jog with Hermes, followed by Doxy and Andy,

Trent put the last dog in its kennel at the same time Deputy Johnson's Jeep rumbled to a stop.

Trent jogged across the parking lot, sliding to a stop when a German Shepherd in a black K-9 vest jumped from the back seat with an agile leap.

"Is that Sarge?"

"Yeah." Christian made a hand motion and Sarge fell into step at his handler's knee. "Jacobson's had me working with him. Seems I have a partner whether I wanted one or not."

"He's looking good." Trent nodded his head toward the dog, knowing better than to approach the animal. His training and protectiveness made him an excellent asset to the police, but it also meant he wasn't a pet. No patting this dog on the head without express permission from his handler.

"You did a fine job training him." Johnson reached out to shake hands and Sarge sniffed the air, his brushy tail wagging slightly. "Mind if we walk around? Been cooped up in the office all day filing reports." He thumbed toward the dog sitting by his leg. "He flunked the Search and Rescue program. Sailed through the bomb and drug class though. Looks like we have a detector dog on the team now."

Trent shrugged and moved toward the shade covering half the building. "Did you bring him to check up on me, or for the exercise?"

"You have anything for a drug dog to detect?" The incredulous lift of his voice and half smile caused Trent to grin.

"Not on your life. Happy to report that's one thing I never did."

"But the rest. The B&Es, the dog fighting. You own up to that."

"It's not something I'm proud of. I don't go around announcing to the world that I made some horrible mistakes more than ten years ago that could have landed me in prison." Trent halted, discomfort tightening his muscles. "Listen, Christian, I know I have no right to ask, but Kara's on her way here, and I'd prefer she not know the dirty details."

"She doesn't know anything?"

"I told her I used to work in a dog fighting ring. But I don't know if she believed me."

"If you're serious about this girl, you gotta tell her." He clapped a hand to Trent's shoulder, the gesture familiar and somewhat comforting. "You look at her like she's made of gold. There's nothing worse than learning your partner's darkest secrets. She deserves to know now. Not later."

Not like how Christian learned the woman he'd loved for years only told him she'd never wanted kids until after their daughter was born. After she packed her bags and booked a ride to the mainland, ready to leave her newborn daughter behind.

"I'm not interested in Kara like that. I'm her boss."

"Keep telling yourself that. Maybe one day you'll believe it." Johnson helped himself to the obstacle course, sending Sarge over the rope bridge and through the tunnel with a flick of his hand. "You said one of them called you. You know who?"

"Snake. Not the main guy, but higher up the pecking order than I ever managed."

"You think he'll come for you? Come after this place? Georgia police never found them or the fighting ring. This could be our chance."

"You think I should invite him over for coffee and donuts?" Trent gave his head a hard shake. "You don't know these men like I do."

"So tell me what I don't know. You spent the biggest part of a year on the mainland with them before you came back here and busted into Pop's house. Again. First time must not have taught you anything. All those months shoveling manure as restitution didn't do anything but fill your head with dreams of big money."

"I made a mistake."

"Sure did. You'd probably still be out there if Pop hadn't

caught you and tossed you in a cell." Johnson rewarded Sarge with a KONG chew toy and the dog bounded away to gnaw his favorite toy. "I'll never understand how he could let you go. Twice."

Trent didn't know either. Christian's dad had hauled him into the police station and let him stew in a cell for a couple hours both times Trent broke into the older man's modest home. Instead of pressing charges, he'd let Trent go. But the look of disappointment on his face...it still caused shame.

"I wouldn't still be with them." Trent traced the scar on his arm, remembering. "I'd be dead if your dad hadn't intervened that night."

"Your girl's here." Johnson jerked his head, his eyebrows lifting in an appreciative tilt. "You say you're not interested, mind if I take a shot?"

"Thought you'd sworn off women?"

"They can't all be like Sarah." His ex-fiancée's name fell out of his mouth like a curse.

"Knock yourself out." *Please.* Trent ignored the sudden burn in his gut. Probably acid reflux. Shouldn't have eaten that whole pizza by himself.

In full deputy mode, Johnson straightened his spine, a move intended to draw attention to the fact he worked out several times a week and had the muscles to prove it, then took a hurried step toward Kara. "Afternoon. I was wondering if you'd like to have coffee with me one morning?"

Kara flushed, pink sparking across her cheeks, even as her gaze traveled over Johnson's puffed out chest. "No, thanks."

He deflated, slumping forward like a child denied his favorite toy. "Well. If you ever change your mind, give me a call." He passed over his business card, embossed with Mimosa's police decal.

Kara slipped the card into her back pocket and nodded toward the building. "I'll go on inside and get started."

Trent loved her for her ability to keep out of his personal business. No doubt she'd be curious why a deputy was here again. But instead of hovering, she darted into the building at a quick trot. Trying to escape? Him or Johnson? And why did it matter that she might be running from him?

"I've never seen you back down that fast. What's wrong? Lost your game?" Trent punched Johnson's shoulder before remembering Sarge might take offense to his human being hit. The dog lay quiet, alert but unimpressed with Trent's actions.

"I thought it might be time to get back in the game." Wincing, Christian rubbed the back of his neck. "I was wrong." Calling for Sarge, he tapped Trent's shoulder with one finger. "If he calls back, you let me know. I have a feeling this isn't over. When he finds out what you have here, Snake won't be able to resist. A former member as a supplier? That's too good a deal."

"Sure." Trent rolled his shoulders to fight the knots. "How's your daughter?"

Christian's face creased into a wide smile. "More beautiful every day." He bobbed his head toward the building. "Remember what I said."

Trent let Christian walk away without answering. He had no reply. Whether he answered Snake's call a second time depended on his mood when the phone rang. He had enough on his plate to keep him busy from daylight till dark for the next two months. With October closing in fast, his hair-brained idea for a Christmas adoption, and the sunup to sundown work at the shelter, he needed his head examined for even considering taking on more work.

One thing he'd say about Christmas, it snuck up on an unprepared man. And if this adoption thing was going to work out, any distractions needed to be sent packing.

Excluding Kara. That distraction he needed. Like a cavity-filled mouth needed a bucket of ice cream. Although it might hurt him in the long run, the instant gratification was worth the pain.

He found her in his office, her sandal-clad feet on his desk and her hair cascading over the back of the chair in golden waves. Relaxed, serious, but with a charm that radiated to those around her.

"I hope I didn't pull you away from anything important."

Her feet hit the floor, the thud echoing. "Family get together, but it was ending anyway, so no worries." Kara waved her hand, her first sign of agitation.

"Why'd you say no to Christian?" Ouch. Trent gave an inward sigh. *Didn't mean to ask that. Now she'll think you're interested.* He strove for a nonchalant shrug. "I mean, not many women say no to a guy like him." Okay. That made it worse.

"Then he won't be upset at missing out on a miserable date with me." Kara combed her hair into a ponytail, leaving him with a sudden urge to beg her to leave it down. He liked this Kara. The one who relaxed in his office and didn't appear to have a care in the world. Except, he peered closer, eying the fine lines pinching her mouth. Even this Kara had something lurking behind that careful gaze.

Focus. He needed to focus. On something other than the way Kara nibbled on a pencil like a rabbit.

8

*H*e needed to stop looking at her like that. Kara rolled the pencil between her fingers and cleared her throat. "What are you thinking for adoption day? When? Where? Do you have anything already in mind that you feel you absolutely must have?"

There. Her voice rang through, clear and concise, without a hint of the tremor shaking her bones at Trent's melting gaze.

"Uh…The week before Christmas would be okay. I'll offer to keep the adopted animals here until the parents wanted to pick them up. No sense ruining the surprise by having to take a puppy home a week early."

"What if we do a carnival? A Christmas carnival? All the mobile businesses could come. Oh, and my grandmother makes *the best* knitted sweaters. If people have a reason to bring their kids, other than to see puppies, they'll be more likely to show up. Who doesn't want to see Beth for a dinner plate, then stop by Mallory's for a new book? Then, 'Oh, look! Puppies!' And the kids get to play while you tell them about the adoptions. It's a win-win."

"You're a genius." Trent fell into the chair across from her, the seat she normally occupied when they met for morning meetings and decided who to photograph and put on the website each day. "I've never heard you talk that long at once."

"You listen. It's easy to talk when someone actually pays attention."

"I've always paid attention to you." His head snapped up, eyes giving off a spark of anger.

There you go, saying what you think again.

"Yes. You do. When I ask which animal is next, you tell me. But you never attempt to engage me in conversation beyond what we're doing in that moment." *Shut up, Kara!* Pressing her lips together, she held back the flood of words begging to be said.

"I—" Trent jerked his head in a nod that sent his hair slapping against his forehead. "Who should we put on the poster?"

And that's how you ruin a good thing. "Remus and Romulus are your best attraction. They're young and playful while giving that hint of responsibility. You want to make sure the parents know what they're getting into by adopting a puppy. We don't want them coming back in January asking to return the animals." We. Why did that one word hold such meaning? Forever Pals belonged to Trent. No *we*.

"What camera do you need?"

The question sent Kara rearing back in the chair until the front wheels threatened to leave the ground.

"I told you I'd replace your camera. Now, show me what you want." Trent indicated the computer occupying a small corner of his desk with a wave of his hand, knocking over a stack of invoices and sending an array of papers fluttering to the ground. His groan ended in mid-voice. "Knew I'd better put those up while I had the chance." He motioned at the computer again before dropping to the floor. "Camera. Show me."

"Trent, you really don't—"

"I pay my debts, Kara. Either find the one you want, or I'll find one for you. And I know nothing about cameras, so keep that in mind." He tapped the papers together against the floor, never looking up.

Muttering, Kara fired up the computer and waited for the usual stream of updates before opening a browser and typing in the specs for the camera she'd lost. Trent moved behind her, his stomach brushing her shoulder in the tight confines of his office. Her fingers jumped across the keys, typing in a string of nonsense that she had to backspace.

Had the room shrunk?

She twitched her body forward, attempting to make the move natural. When Trent's breath danced across the back of her neck and sent shivers of delight down her spine, she shot up from the chair, clipping his chin with her shoulder in the process. "I'll be outside."

She couldn't breathe. Air. Needed air.

Phone in hand and dialing before Trent had time to call her back, Kara dialed Mel's number and stepped into the cool relief of early afternoon. Blood whooshed through her head and obliterated most of Mel's greeting.

"Were you at the shelter this morning?" Kara stammered through the question and knocked her fist against her forehead.

"Why? Has something happened?"

"Did you tell Trent to call me?"

"I think you need to start at the beginning. You're not making any sense."

Kara slapped her ponytail over her shoulder, tucked herself against the trunk of a fallen loblolly pine that the hurricane had ripped apart, and filled Mel in on the last hour. From Trent's call, to arriving as Christian left, and Trent's idea for the Christmas adoption, the words fell out faster and faster. She finished with, "He should have called Pen."

Mel remained silent so long that Kara checked her phone to see if the call had dropped. The brush at the edge of the parking lot rustled, jerking Kara to her feet. She had enough time to bunch her hand into a fist when Mel emerged, ducking under the foliage and tucking her phone into her shorts pocket.

"You look tense. Relax." Mel's grin became sly, almost contemplative. "Are you complaining about Trent because he asked you to do the job or because he believes you can do it?"

"What's that supposed to mean?" Hands on hips, Kara confronted Mel long enough to see the gleam in her friend's eyes grow to new bounds.

"You've worked here, what, a year now? I've seen your work. Watched you work. You're an exceptional photographer who's wasting her talents on a tiny island and, from what I can see, has about as much faith in herself as a poodle does of becoming a Doberman."

"That's a long assessment."

"Yeah, well." Mel cleared her throat. "I tend to jump to conclusions, so my goal for this year was to become more in tune with people. To see them for who they are instead of who I *think* they are. Tell me I'm wrong, and I'll take back everything I said."

Zeke popped out from the bushes and wrapped his arms around Mel, causing her to squeal when he hauled her backward off her feet. She slapped his forearms. "Make yourself useful. Go help Trent get the animals put away for the night."

"You're never going to get tired of sending me in there, are you?" Zeke gave a dramatic sigh before he kissed Mel's cheek and retracted his arms. Walking by Kara, he nodded. "Kara. Nice to see you again."

She returned the gesture before turning a glare at Mel. "What are you doing here? We were on the phone, then poof, you're here." If the brittle hostility surprised Mel, she didn't show it. Why was Kara trying to make an enemy of Mel? The question rattled against Kara's shattered confidence.

"Zeke and I were walking the pups when you called. Since

we were halfway here, I came ahead while he took the dogs home. I needed to see Trent anyway, to make sure he's coming to the fall festival next weekend." Mel stripped a piece of bark from a nearby tree and began shredding it into tiny pieces. "You're coming, right?"

"Should be fun." In her dreams, perhaps. In reality, a party the size of the fall festival amounted to visiting the dentist for eight hours. The interaction would leave her disoriented and wishing she'd canceled. But it was the first big event on Hopper after the hurricane, and everyone was expected. Distract and redirect. "What are you going to wear?"

Given that singular opportunity, Mel launched into a detailed account of her and Zeke's costumes. Kara nodded and agreed when appropriate that yes, the costumes would be wonderful. No, she doubted anyone else would wear the same thing.

Why did you agree to plan a festival? The thought ran circles around her mind, setting off a frenzy of insecurities.

"When are you going to ask me to help?" Mel's question popped the bubble of doubt and brought an entirely new threat.

Help with what?

"I wasn't planning on asking anyone to help with anything." Well, now that came off as arrogant. Kara's cheeks flamed, something the gathering darkness hid from Mel. "I didn't mean that the way it sounded."

"Don't worry." Mel swatted the air as though mosquitoes plagued her. "I do the same thing. Seriously, though. You intend to plan, coordinate, and execute the entire carnival without anyone's help? I'm all for being self-sufficient and indepen-dent...but I don't think any one person could pull that off alone."

True. What *had* been her plan for this crazy idea Trent talked her into? The thought of calling people and asking them to help made her itch. What then? If they did agree, the workload lessened, but her anxiety rose tenfold. They'd look to her for direction, for orders.

"I think I've made a terrible mistake." She started to turn away, to run into the building and tell Trent to find someone else. Anyone else. Mel, for one.

"You can do this, you know." Mel's quiet reassurance stopped Kara. "I know it's outside your comfort zone, but I believe in you. And, for the record, I'd love to help."

"You'll make all the calls and tell everyone what needs to be done?" Her own hopeful tone sounded pathetic to her ears. Pawning off her responsibility seemed such a cop-out when Mel had her own business to run and a wedding to plan.

"Afraid not, but I will help. And so will others. This isn't all on you. But you will have to tell us what you need. Even if what you need is a break from all of us."

Be brave, Kara. Could she? Was it possible for someone as insecure and introverted as her to step out of the comfortable shadows? She had to try. For Trent. For *herself.*

Lord, will You help me?

9

*S*unday morning after church, Trent plodded across the parking lot. Kara stood on the outskirts of a large group. With her arms clasped tightly over her stomach, she gave off an intense vibe of wishing to be anywhere else.

Tossing caution to the wind, he approached. "Great service this morning."

Kara nodded and twitched toward an elderly woman who apparently believed thumping people's knees with a cane a great pastime. Spotting Kara, the rheumy eyes developed a sudden spark, and she hobbled her way through the crowd, whacking legs and cackling as she passed.

"Kara dear, who's your friend?" Feeble though she looked, her voice cracked loud enough to draw the attention of a large portion of the group.

"Granny, this is Trent, my boss."

"The one who called you in the middle of a family dinner? The one you skedaddled away like a frog in a pot of hot water for?" Eyes dancing with obvious delight, Kara's grandmother tapped the ground with her cane. "I understand your rush."

"Granny!"

"Don't you *Granny* me. It's about time you found a nice young man."

Trent bit back a laugh. Knowing Kara as he did, the attention was unwelcome. He risked a touch to her lower back and regretted it when the shrewd eyes tracked his movement. Removing his hand and clearing his throat, Trent brushed a hand through his hair. "Well, I'll take that as my cue to skedaddle. I'll talk to you tomorrow."

Not quite running but walking at a faster pace than considered polite, he escaped, making it all the way to his truck before Kara called his name. He debated ignoring the soft voice for only a second before he turned.

"Did you need me for something?"

Did he? His reasoning for invading the familial unit seemed flimsy now that he'd taken a step away from the situation. "How's the planning going?" When her expression went from hopeful to closed off, he wanted to smack himself.

"Mel's agreed to help when she has time. I'll start making calls tomorrow for the rest of the committee and see who's interested in setting up a booth."

"Let me know if there's anything I can do to help. This is a mutual project, after all." He forced his mouth into a smile before reaching for the truck door. "Enjoy the rest of your day."

"Yeah. Same."

After drying his clammy hands on his jeans, Trent cranked the engine and set out for the far side of Hopper. The glimpse he'd caught of his dad on the front pew this morning drove him to check in. His pounding pulse and sweating temple spoke of greater problems coming his way. He'd waited too long, let the perceived tension corrode his confidence.

He passed the wreckage Hopper still needed to overcome. The uprooted trees and houses without roofs, all with the permanence of hope showing through in sprigs of green grass and the joyful expressions on the faces he drove past.

His life resembled the mess. The mistakes he'd made lay across his path like the uprooted trees left to rot, blocking him from moving forward with a new life.

Time to take an excavator to the debris. Tree stump by tree stump, if need be.

Rolling down his window allowed the salt-tinged air to clear his muddled thoughts. This bright new day begged for hope and life, happiness, and joy.

His dad's cottage came into view, shooting up from the tall grasses and sand. Jeremy Raines lived his life the same way he preached it. Love. Forgiveness. And without many of the simple creature comforts that most considered normal. The existence Trent had rebelled against as a teen but learned to appreciate as experience softened his desires.

Trent killed the engine, slid from the truck, and approached the front door after wiping his palms over his jeans one last time. The gruff "come in" drew Trent back more than a dozen years. To the first time he'd ever felt the need to knock on this door. The night it stopped feeling like home because he no longer deserved the love his dad had always shown him.

"How many times I have to tell you, you don't have to knock. Doesn't matter where you live, this is your home, too." With a shake of his head, his dad continued. "No sense standing out there." He pushed the screen door open with a screech of rusty hinges.

"Hi, Dad."

"Didn't know you'd be stopping by or I'd have fixed lunch." Wrapping one arm around Trent's neck in their customary embrace, he patted Trent's shoulder with a strong thump.

"I can't stay long. Came to see how you're doing."

"Same as always. Getting older, grayer, and less inclined to go scuba diving."

"You've never been scuba diving."

"And I'm less inclined to start now." Nudging Trent toward

the couch, his dad returned to his faithful recliner. "What brings you by here? Not that I'm not happy to see you, but I can tell from your face this is more than a mercy call on your old man."

Shoot. He'd meant to keep his face from telling so much, but after years behind the pulpit, his dad read people the way most read words.

"Snake called." Trent waited for the recriminations. The questions.

"This the same fella who you fell in with before? I heard about the break-ins on Mimosa. That his doing?"

A breath of relief hissed out. No judgments or insinuations that Trent himself had fallen back into bad habits let him lift his gaze from the floor and stare his dad in the eye.

"You expected me to think you'd gone back to that life? To accuse you?" Shaking his gray-streaked head, his dad gripped the recliner arms and leaned forward. "Son, I don't know why you keep expecting me to think the worst of you. Maybe because you always expect the worst of yourself. But I never have. You made mistakes. I forgave you for them. God forgave you for them. Johnson forgave you. He made you pay back the damages, but he forgave you. The only one still holding on to your past is you."

"I don't mean to."

"Takes time to make changes. Especially when you keep flogging yourself. Hard to move forward when you chain yourself to the past. But we know a God who breaks those chains and leaves the cell door wide open. If we never walk through it, well, then that's our fault, isn't it?" Hands folded over his stomach, the man who'd raised Trent, loved him, and prayed unceasingly for his soul still had the ability to shred every argument.

Needing time to digest his dad's message, Trent stood and rushed toward the kitchen. "You know what, I'm hungry. How about I cook us some lunch?"

The recliner squeaked as his dad pulled the lever that lifted the footrest, the sound as familiar as Trent's own heartbeat and as certain an agreement as he'd get.

His hand slid off the refrigerator door handle, his sweat-slick palms forcing him to wipe them off once again on his jeans.

In the years since he moved out, nothing in the house had changed. His dad still cooked on the stove he'd bought back in the seventies when he and his bride set up house.

His mother's touch lingered in the lace curtains and doilies draped over every table though she'd been gone for fifteen years. The old anger flickered only to be smothered by guilt at the sight of a centerpiece she'd made, the flowers so old and faded they no longer resembled their original color, that still graced the center of the square table.

Trent raked his fingers over the nicked and stained wood. How many hours had he sat here, doing homework or listening as Dad muttered over his Bible reading and scratched out notes with a knife-sharpened pencil? While cancer stole his mom all those years ago and his dad buried himself in work, Trent lost his tether, allowing the anger to carry him away to a land where wrong seemed okay and right no longer mattered.

Ringing penetrated the fog of memory and drew Trent's hand to his pocket.

Snake.

Trent saved the number after that first call, wanting to have the option of not answering. Johnson's request drove Trent's finger to hover over the green button. He slid it across and lifted the phone.

"I'm going to assume you didn't mean to hang up on me yesterday. Because if you did, then our friendship is heading down a dark path."

"We never had a friendship." Trent hardened his tone, infusing all the anger into his voice. "You used me then, and I expect you want to use me now. Let me help you out. Whatever you want from me, the answer is no."

"That's too bad." Snake's hiss spread, insisting on causing tension. "I believe you're in a rare position to make a lot of money with almost no effort. Seems a man living with nearly nothing might be curious about my offer."

Trent opened his mouth, intending to ask how Snake knew anything about how or where Trent lived. The phone in his hand had gone silent.

As Sherlock Holmes would say, "The game is afoot" and Snake's game held disastrous consequences for everyone involved.

*K*ara spent more time than she'd like to admit debating whether to call in sick on Monday morning.

Trent had plenty of employees to help him. What did he need her for? Pictures. A scoff burned up her throat before the sad eyes of a puppy she'd photographed last week chased away her foul mood.

After one last glance in the mirror and a scowl at her reflection, she headed to Forever Pals with her spare camera tucked away in her backpack.

Trent met her at the front door, holding it open as he ushered her inside.

Anticipation bubbled in her stomach, churning the single cup of coffee it contained into a frothy mess. When he didn't mention their meeting after church the day before, Kara let her disappointment trail along like a misbehaving pup. "Who's first this morning?"

Trent's surprised gaze roved her face before landing on her backpack. "You have another camera?"

"Not a good one, but it'll do the job until my new one

arrives. I'll need more time with the dogs though, to get the perfect shot." She hitched the strap higher on her shoulder and tightened her grip. "I'll go set up."

She scuttled down the hall and into the room they'd created, able to breathe again once out of Trent's presence. *What is wrong with you? It's Trent! You've worked together for a year, so why the sudden pre-adolescent jitters?*

By the time Trent arrived with a stack of index cards in his hands, her nerves were back where they belonged, and she even managed to smile when he handed over his notes.

Kara read over the first card. Female Chihuahua. Name: Peony. Color: Tan. Three years old. Needs a single pet home, possibly with an elderly couple.

"Is she playful at all?"

"Not that I've seen. Peony's a nervous sort, but thankfully not yappy."

"All right." Kara began tossing items into her makeshift studio which, for a dog Peony's size, consisted of a large box draped in fabric. She swapped out the black cotton for a Christmas red. "I'm almost ready."

Trent backed out of the room.

She had no more than ten minutes before he'd return with Peony. Strapping the camera around her neck and throwing an elf hat into the box, Kara snapped a test shot to check the lighting. Abysmal.

A low whine announced Peony's arrival. Trent crooned to the shaking canine wrapped in his capable arms. As his thumb rubbed the dog's head, Kara flicked the curtains open at the same time her finger depressed the shutter button.

"Working on landscapes now too?"

She startled at Trent's voice, her body coming alive at the tone he reserved for scared animals. The contradiction of emotion needed a heavy dose of reality. "You never know, that might be my best picture yet."

He chuckled.

Kara turned in time to watch him lower Peony into the box. He continued patting the dog's head, and the slightly bulging eyes closed as his touch soothed and comforted.

"How did you work in a dog fighting ring?" Despite all her best efforts, forgetting Trent's admission had been impossible. Asking him here, now, while he focused on a nervous dog and couldn't become angry seemed like an excellent idea.

"By being young, stupid, and naïve enough to believe that quick and easy money meant I wouldn't have to get my hands dirty." His thumb stroked Peony's ear, but his head lifted and his eyes locked onto hers. "My first fight, one of the dogs didn't want to go into the ring, so Snake tried to convince the dog that being inside was better than staying outside."

"Is that how you got bit?"

Trent jerked his head, his expression morphing into one of shame and guilt. His eyes lost their shine while his shoulders slumped. Peony licked his palm, drawing a tilt to his lips. "Peony's ready."

In other words, no more questions.

With great effort, she shifted focus from interrogation to photography. Peony nestled into the soft, red fabric until only her face peeked out. Kara squatted and brought the camera to her eye. "See if you can get the hat on."

Trent did as she asked, setting the elf hat on Peony's head with a gentle hand, while Kara watched through the camera lens. The moment he let go, she held the shutter button. Rapid-fire clicks filled the silence until Peony shook her head, knocking the green and red felt hat to the floor.

Kara switched to view mode and scanned the photos. "We're good."

They continued this way for hours. Speaking only when necessary and no more than required. With each animal coming through her "studio," the anger and tension tightening the muscles along her spine increased.

"Let's break for lunch."

Settling her camera into its slot in the backpack, Kara rolled her shoulders and rocked her head from side to side. The tight muscles eased, but only enough to stop the threat of a headache.

Trent started to leave the room, then paused when Kara slid down the wall and sat on the floor. He hesitated, the Labrador's leash in his hand. The chocolate lab had been her favorite of the morning with its playful antics and doggy smile.

Kara crossed her arms over her stomach and leaned her head against the cold concrete windowsill.

The door clicked behind Trent as he led the dog back to its cage.

Names floated across her vision when she closed her eyes. People she needed to call and ask about joining her in planning the festival. Potential venders. Rental equipment.

"What's wrong?"

Heat spread across her knee, and she opened her eyes to Trent's hand settled there. Something in her face must have told him she approved, because he squeezed with enough pressure to reassure without triggering a ticklish response.

"I don't think I can do it." The words hurtled out of her mouth, firing like the clicks of her camera on multi-shot mode.

"I need more to go on than that." Trent sat beside her, his hand never leaving her leg.

"The festival. Calling people. Ordering people around when it's time to start setting things up. I can't do it. Calling and asking them if they want to participate makes my palms sweat." Her fingers tightened on the t-shirt she'd thrown on. No sense wearing pretty clothes when they'd be covered in dog hair by the end of the day.

"I can—" A series of yowls interrupted Trent. The door opened, a white muzzle nudging into the space where Trent had failed to properly ensure the latch engaged. Remus bounded into the room, Romulus on his tail and gnawing on something that resembled a wallet.

"Romulus!" Trent dodged Remus' tongue and reached for the strip of black leather. "Where'd you get that?" He pulled the slobbery mess from the dog's mouth and gave Remus a gentle shove in Kara's direction.

Remus took Trent's motion as permission and crawled into Kara's lap, where he proceeded to yowl at her before planting his paws on her shoulders and giving her face a thorough bathing. Laughing, Kara pushed the exuberant pup back onto his haunches. "Down, Remus."

The dog sat for all of three seconds before bounding up and snapping at Romulus' tail. The two pups scrabbled across the floor, their claws clicking a mad tune of playful instrumentals.

Trent pulled bits of sopping paper from the shredded wallet. Retrieving the driver's license, his shoulders stiffened. "This is Snake's wallet."

"You're sure? How did it get here?" The churning in her gut returned, this time an angry convergence of fear and anxiety.

"I have to call Christian. He needs to know Snake's been on the Island." He nudged her shoulder and glared at the rowdy canines. "You sure you want these two as poster boys for the carnival? They're as likely to eat your camera as to let you get a decent picture."

Kara sniggered and clapped a hand over her mouth, her tension dissolving. "They're exactly what we need. As soon as Zeke builds me a sleigh and you figure out a way to make it snow."

"Snow? You want snow...on an island where the temperatures never even get close to freezing?"

"I never said it would be easy. Or that the snow had to be real. Come on, Trent. Live a little." She nudged him. "Can you imagine the excitement, the pure joy on the kids' faces when they see snow? Half the islanders have probably never seen it before."

Romulus yipped and lowered his front paws to the ground while his back end stuck straight up into the air. His brushy tail waved back and forth, and he threw his head to the side in a long howl.

"Okay. Okay. I hear you." Trent tapped the pup's nose, sending Romulus running around the room until he lost traction and slid sideways against Trent's leg. "What am I going to do with you, huh?" He ruffled furry ears and glanced at Kara. "You're smiling. You haven't smiled all day. I've missed it."

Remus jumped and licked her chin as though he agreed with Trent that her smile was something to be missed.

"I'll help you with the carnival. I never meant for you to think you had to do everything alone." His knee brushed hers, then came back to rest with an easy pressure, sending a spark along the nerves and straight to her pitter-pattering heart.

Funny how the romance novels had it so right and so wrong all at the same time.

The barn had been transformed into an explosion of
fall colors and scents. Trent adjusted his Where's
Waldo hat and slid through the crowd. The boldly striped red
and white shirt left him sticking out like a Great Pyrenees in a
Pug contest.

A knot of people cut him off from his intended target. He
nodded at the ones he recognized, commented on the crafts-
manship of a hand-sewn costume, and wiggled away in search
of his quarry.

Where'd she go? There. A flash of blue and yellow.

Kara skirted the edges of the party, her denim overalls and
plaid shirt much more conducive to getting lost amid the
throng. The scarecrow makeup made him overlook her the first
time he scanned the massive space.

"Hey, Trent, isn't it supposed to be hard to find Waldo?
You've made it too easy."

Trent smiled at the kid from the youth group and shrugged.
"I'm surprised you even know who Waldo is."

"Grandpa hates TV. Says it rots our brains. I spend an hour

or two on a puzzle of Where's Waldo every time I drop by to visit." The kid laughed, and Trent joined in with a smile.

A girl about the same age joined them. With bright red cheeks and a miserable twist to her mouth, she mumbled, "You wanna dance?"

In a flash, the boy's face turned crimson. He'd never seen a kid blush so fast. Chuckling as he turned away, Trent returned to the hunt.

One more nudge, a shimmy between two separate groups, and Trent closed the gap as the music shifted from upbeat to a slow melody.

"Would you like to dance?" Several people turned to stare.

Kara froze in mid-step between light and shadow.

His voice must have carried further than he intended. "Please." He tilted his head. "One dance. If Mel doesn't see me on the dance floor at least once, she'll hound me for days."

"I fail to see how that's my problem." Her lips twitched, drawing her scarecrow smile wide.

Trent held out his hand and wiggled both eyebrows. He liked this Kara. The one who had a bit of humor and sass and spoke more than three words stacked together. He'd lured her in, now to make her stay. "Because if you say no, I'm going to tell Mel you turned me down, and I was so brokenhearted that I couldn't bear to ask anyone else."

Kara tossed her head back and laughed, rustling the straw hair stuffed in the layers between the oversized hat and her own blonde strands. "Flattery will get you nowhere, but I do love this song."

She slid her palm against his. Tugging gently, Trent led her to the dance floor and spun her into his embrace. Her laugh brushed over his ear, and his hands tightened around her waist.

Music had the ability to draw emotion, to let it flow with ease. But this, holding Kara in his arms for the first time, turned into a song so deep and resonant his heart ached.

This—each beat growing stronger and the heat spreading from her touch on his shoulders—this is what he'd been waiting for. An undeniable realization that *this woman* held the other half of him.

Trent lost himself to the moment, the sway of limbs and climbing intensity. He shifted forward, asking Kara to meet him, and her cheek lowered to his shoulder. The hat's brim grazed his jaw, preventing Trent from lowering his head. This would be enough. For now.

As the final chord died away, Kara lifted her head, her gaze shooting up to meet his. Her hands fluttered over his shoulders, no doubt expecting him to release her, but he couldn't. Not yet.

Kara's breath stuttered when he dipped his head, but instead of moving closer, she nudged his shoulder and cleared her throat. "Better go ask those other girls to dance now that I've not turned you down. You've no excuse."

"Who says I want to ask anyone else?" He dropped his hands but remained in the same spot.

As the scent of cider tickled his nose, Kara wrinkled hers. "You shouldn't say things you don't mean." She strode away, leaving him on the edge of the dance floor with empty arms and an even emptier heart.

After the third *what's-eating-you?* glare from Mel, Trent slipped outside, ducking behind the barn and into the quiet night. Setting his back against the firm wall, he let the dance move through him again, relishing each moment, until a quiet hiss jerked him back to the rustle of trees and pine permeating the air.

"Trent? What are you doing out here?" Mel slid alongside him, her arms crossed.

"Me? What about you? You'll ruin your dress. And where's Zeke?"

"He's waiting around the corner." Mel buffed her arms and

shivered even though the temperature remained mild. "I saw you dancing with Kara."

"And now you're out here, stalking me, when you should be in there"—he thumbed the barn and grinned—"enjoying a night of whispered promises and slow dances with your fiancé."

He could *feel* Mel's frown as she poked his shoulder. "Fine. I'll go. I came out here to make sure you're all right. Excuse me for caring." Her breath caught mid huff and turned to laughter. "I'm sorry. I can't stay mad at you. But I really do care, so call if you need me." She sauntered away, her pink dress floating above the ground and the gold braid around her waist flashing in a glint of moonlight.

"Should I address Zeke as Wesley or Dread Pirate Roberts when I see him at the wedding?"

"You recognize our costumes?" Mel whirled, her hands patting the material around her legs. "I was afraid no one would figure it out."

"Come on, have a little faith. *The Princess Bride?* That one was easy. It's Mallory I can't figure out." Trent gave Mel's shoulder a gentle push. "Go back inside. I'm fine. I think I'll head home."

He strode away from the party, ensuring Mel's return to Zeke and the festivities she loved.

He knew where he wanted to be, and since he couldn't bring himself to follow her like some stalker, he settled for the second-best thing. In a matter of minutes, he was steering his truck toward the ocean, tires brushing the coastline until the shadow of Forever Pals beckoned in the distance.

Another vehicle sat in the lot. Trent let the truck roll to a stop and waited, thumbs tapping a slow beat on the steering wheel. To leave or not to leave? That question threatened to set his world ablaze or drown him in sorrow.

Muttering beneath his breath about the injustice of poetry, Trent slid from the truck and approached Kara's window.

Her rigid posture told him to leave, but the quiet movement of her shoulders demanded he stay.

He hovered at her window, bordering between the lines of creepy she's-going-to-scream-when-she-sees-you and sincere don't-scare-the-girl-to-death. His soft tap caused her to jerk in his direction as her hands flew into defensive fists.

"Easy, Daisy, lower them dukes."

As soon as she recognized him in the harsh light of the nearby streetlamp, Kara lowered her hands and rolled down the window with the press of a button. "You sneak up on a girl in the middle of the night in a dark parking lot, you better be glad you didn't get maced." She let out a shuddering breath. "What are you doing here?"

"Well, this is my building." He strove for a nonchalant expression, but the feeling of his cheeks pinching and Kara's sudden interest in her fingernails said he failed miserably. "Did you leave something inside?"

"No..." She blew out a breath and started to swipe her hand over her cheeks, only to stop with a frown. "Needed somewhere to think."

No way he'd try and puzzle that one out. "You want to come inside?"

"It's getting late. I should head home." Rolling up the window, Kara gave a miniature salute and flicked on her headlights before shifting into drive.

Trent turned his back. He had to. It was either feign indifference or chase after her car like a misbehaving canine. The idea had merit, except he'd likely end up as squashed as those poor dogs.

"You've been holding out on me." Spoken from the darkness like the slime he was, Snake hissed and strode into view, following the path that led around to the obstacle course and eventually to Trent's home. "I was about to introduce myself to your girl when you showed up." He grinned, a slow, predatory smile. "There's plenty of time for that. *After* we finish our business here."

"We have no business here, Snake. I want you off this property, and off the Islands. Get back to the mainland where you belong."

"And if I don't." He pressed closer, the stench of body odor threatening the contents of Trent's stomach.

"I'm not afraid of you. Not anymore. And this time, I'm not worried about who the law will believe." He waved his phone under Snake's nose. "I'm not that kid anymore. Get off my property."

Snake spit a glob of mucus onto the pavement at Trent's feet. "You forget yourself, hotshot. This here is public property. You can't make me leave."

"Oh, but I can." Trent balled his hands into fists, briefly forgetting the phone until the hard edges pressed into his palm.

"We'll see. Keep an eye on that girl of yours. Be a shame if something happened to her." Snake backed away, hands in the air. But this was not surrender. The gleam of teeth and barking laughter said Trent had only added fuel to the fire.

Trent tapped out a text to Christian, telling him of Snake's appearance and threat to Kara. Christian responded with a police car emoji and a promise to check in with Kara after Thanksgiving. The warning would come better from him.

What if? Trent rubbed a hand over his chest, where his rapid heartbeat attempted to settle. What if he'd not shown up? *God, I don't know what to do. Every time I try to move forward, I get pulled back.*

*a*fter a wonderful Thanksgiving meal at her parents' house, Kara flopped into her office chair and moaned. Full belly. An exciting day filled with interactions and family. Exhaustion didn't begin to cover the fatigue tugging at her muscles.

Kara tapped her pencil on the desk while rubbing her eyes and muttering at the stack of lists littering every available space. *Why are you making this such a big deal?*

Her resounding snort sent a sheet of paper covered in indecipherable scribbles fluttering across the wooden desk and onto the floor. When her phone rang, she lunged for it as though it had all the answers to life's dilemmas.

Mel's face blipped across the screen and her voice bounced with energy when Kara took the call. "Hey, so, I've a question. If I were to bring a couple people to your house to work on setting up the Christmas festival...how many is too many? People, that is?"

"What are you talking about?" Kara pushed back from the desk and let her chair accept the full weight of her collapse. "What people? When?"

"Well..."

The pause sent Kara's head reeling. "You're here now. Aren't you?"

"I should have called earlier. I'm sorry! We can leave."

"I'll meet you at the door." Kara ended the call and let the phone drop with a resounding *plonk*. At least she still had on normal clothes, even if the waistband on her jeans had gotten tight after an extra slice of apple pie. Shoving her hair into a ponytail, she marched toward the door, desperate to prove these women were welcome in her home.

She flung open the door, ready to force her lips into a welcoming smile, and found herself swamped in Mel's hug while Darcy and another woman waved from the edge of the porch.

"You're sure you don't mind? We were planning some last-minute wedding details and the festival came up and, well, things sort of grew legs and ran your way." Mel squeezed Kara's shoulders and leaned back far enough to look into her eyes.

"It's fine." Her voice squeaked, and Kara cleared her throat while backing away and running her hands over her thighs. "Come on in. I have all my stuff in the office."

The three women filed past, each one giving soft smiles and oozing the confidence Kara wished she could find in a bottle to splash on every morning with her Mango Mist body lotion.

"Straight down the hall, first door on the left. You can't miss it." Closing the door as Darcy slid a gentle hand over the knitted sweater hanging on the back of the couch, Kara willed her heart to steady and her hands to stop shaking. *You know them, Kara.* Except that last woman. And that unknown sent a flutter through Kara. *Stop being melodramatic. They're your friends.*

Pasting on a smile that probably looked as uncomfortable as it felt, Kara drew her ragged courage around her shoulders and followed the trio into her office.

Mel had already found the stack of advertisements Kara

created. Those had been easy. A quick hour on her laptop and an online order to the printer and boom, done.

"These are all the people who you think might be interested in being vendors?" Darcy held up the sheet of paper lined from top to bottom with names and businesses.

Kara nodded and ran her tongue over her teeth before answering. Could they smell her breath from here? Should have avoided that last cup of coffee. She took a step back, almost leaving the room. "Do you think it's enough?"

"Are you kidding?" Darcy's question shot fireworks through Kara's mind. Had she done something wrong? "It's fantastic, Kara. I never would have thought of bringing in someone to take family portraits."

Kara's sigh sounded harsh in her ears, but the other women seemed oblivious. "I haven't started calling them yet. Still finalizing the list." *Liar. You're too chicken to call them. Afraid they'll all tell you no.*

Darcy's finger ran down the list, and her brow furrowed. "This is a lot of numbers to call. I bet most of them won't answer either. People nowadays rarely pick up random numbers. What if we email them instead? If we don't get enough interest that way, then we'll worry about calling each one."

Email. Why hadn't she thought of that? Her cheeks lit up, the heat emanating from them forced her from the room before they could take notice and ask what was wrong. The last thing she needed was more attention. "Great idea, Darcy. I'll grab us some drinks and we can work up an email list."

She raced into the kitchen, grabbed a stack of glasses and an assortment of drinks from the refrigerator before pausing at the sink. Hands tight on the counter, Kara leaned over and breathed until her lungs relaxed and the room stopped tilting.

When she returned to the office, Darcy had cleared out a space on the floor and the woman Kara didn't recognize sat with a stack of photos in her hands.

"Kara, I forgot to introduce Abby, Zeke's sister. She's visiting for a while, helping me with wedding preparations." Mel flicked her hands toward Abby, who grinned.

Abby shuffled the photos. "Are these yours?"

Kara tilted her head for a better look before recognizing the images from last month's photo shoot at the animal shelter. The outdoor shots were intended to show the athleticism and agility of the dogs, their fun-loving nature and the bright joy that lit soulful eyes. The fact that Trent took up a large portion of the shot had nothing to do with the exercise and everything to do with the admiration she felt every time he handled one of the canines.

"I'll take that as a yes." Abby grinned, the youthful joy and exuberance taking away any possible sting. "He's cute."

Cute? Kara's head shook from side to side against her permission, which drew Abby's and then Mel's attention.

"I knew it." Mel fist-pumped the air and whooped. "You like Trent. And from what I saw at the barn dance, the feeling is mutual. I've never seen him so out of sorts after a dance. And Zeke worried that Trent had fallen in love with me." Her scoff carried a mixture of laughter and pride.

"Wait. You and Trent?" Abby directed the question at Mel while lurching to her feet and taking the sweating drinks from Kara's hands. "How have I not heard this story?"

"It's nothing." Mel shooed the conversation away. "Not as good as Darcy and Nigel's story."

"Oh no. We are not talking about me and the fact that Nigel *still* hasn't proposed." Darcy's hair whipped from side to side in time with her shaking head. "I've considered asking him myself."

"He'll ask. Be patient." The twinkle in Mel's eye gave away the thrill of a secret.

"What you do know?" Darcy pointed at Mel.

"Nothing! I promise. A feeling. It is almost Christmas. The most romantic time for a proposal."

"Don't get my hopes up any higher than they already are." Darcy warned with a wry twist to her lips. "After that last hike to the lighthouse when I assumed he'd pop the question, I'm done anticipating. It's too hard not to push him overboard when we're on the *Treasure* working."

"You wouldn't do that." Kara covered her mouth after the words escaped.

Darcy's face took on an expression Kara couldn't decipher. "No. I wouldn't. We've had enough scares in the ocean."

How was this supposed to get work done? So far, all they'd accomplished was emptying several bottles of Pepsi and a scattering of papers.

A tense silence wrapped around the room, threatening to strangle the single thread of feminine friendship.

"So, Kara." Mel tapped her finger on the desk. "What can we do to help? You look like you know what you want for the festival. What do you need from us?"

Nothing.

Everything.

Why did she have such a hard time asking for help? *Do it, Kara. One step outside your comfort zone.*

"I need someone to distribute flyers. I'll be at the animal shelter working, and I don't know many people. They'll be more receptive to one of you." She ended on a breathy rush of air, then gulped before the dryness in her throat triggered a cough. *Do You see me, God? Do You hear me? Why do I feel so alone though the room is full?*

"I can do that." Darcy reached for the flyers. "I'm on the ferry every day going back and forth from Mimosa to Elnora. I'll pass them around. Locals only, right? Shouldn't be too hard. Most of the morning crowd are islanders heading in for work."

"What else?" Mel rubbed her hands together and smiled.

"What about social media? Have you made an event site we can share around?"

Kara latched onto the topic and ran, her excitement building to a fever pitch. This she could talk about. Websites and photos and copy edit. She understood this world of language and imagery.

The women around her grabbed blank sheets of paper and began writing, smiles and nods encouraging Kara to soldier on until every thought exhausted itself from her mouth. "I'm sorry. I didn't mean to talk so much."

"Are you kidding?" Mel waved her papers in the air. "This is going to be great. You write up the posts; do what you do best. We'll all help monitor the sites and field any questions. What about a meeting next Friday? We can ask for volunteers."

A heavy knock on her front door sent Kara's hand flying to her chest. She edged toward the door, wishing she'd locked it after letting the women in. Her hand fell on the doorknob as another knock thumped and a deep voice boomed. "Miss Parker? It's Deputy Johnson from Mimosa's Police Department. We met a few days ago. I need to speak with you."

Her hands seemed to take on a life of their own as one clutched her throat and the other jerked the door open to reveal the deputy on the other side.

Mel, Darcy, and Abby shuffled from the office while Christian nodded and stepped inside.

"What's wrong? Is Trent okay?" Kara forced her fingers to relax their grip on her throat, though it did nothing to ease the tension in the air.

"Trent's fine. It's you we're concerned with." Christian hesitated and glanced around the room. "Would you rather speak privately?"

Mel murmured, and the sound of their retreat brought Kara's head around to the now-empty living room. "Looks like here is fine."

"Snake showed up at the animal shelter and threatened you. Nothing specific. But it's best to take the proper precautions."

An angry buzz started in her ears. Kara swatted the noise away, as well as Christian's warning. "It's Trent you should be worried about. That man doesn't care about me." A wiggle of doubt crept in, but she shoved it back down. She had enough to worry about with the adoption day looming overhead.

13

*A*nother Monday morning rolled in with the strength of a steamroller, squashing Trent out flat as he attempted to begin the week.

After an hour of reading his Bible, followed by exercise and a shower, he pulled into Forever Pals and met chaos. A dozen vehicles sat in the parking lot, only one of which he recognized as Kara's.

A knot of people hovered around Kara, who stood with such an expression of misery that Trent jumped from his truck and jogged across the parking lot.

"We're not trying to adopt out your pets." The exasperation leaked from Kara's voice as though she'd said this same sentence over and over. "The festival is to help the *other* pets get adopted. You left your pets here so you could take care of your property after the hurricane. Your pets are safe and sound until you're able to take them home again."

Several people muttered, sounding unconvinced. One man demanded to be let into the building, wanting to see his dog *right now.*

A row of shoulder-to-shoulder, irate islanders blocked the man when he tried to barrel past Kara.

"You take one more step and I'll have the police down here." Steel rang from her tone.

Trent jerked his head in Kara's direction, but her attention remained on the one man who confronted her the loudest.

"You'll all see your pets today. But you'll do it in an orderly fashion, or I'll have you for trespassing, or inciting a riot, or whatever else I can think of before the police arrive. Now back off!" Blue eyes flashing with a spark of authority he didn't know she possessed, Kara crossed her arms and locked her stance. "I know you're worried and upset. You miss your pets, and you want them home. But this is not the way to accomplish that goal. You're all better than this. I watched you pull together after the hurricane. I was at your houses, helping build walls and clean up debris. You don't know me as well as you know Trent, but you *do* know me. And you trust Trent. You entrusted the care of your pets to him, and he won't fail you."

Trent slid through the group, moving to Kara's side as she scanned the crowd. Beneath her crossed arms, her hands gave a violent tremble.

"Okay, people. Let's make a line." Trent clapped his hands, and every head swiveled his direction. "Mary, you and Leonard start us off, would you?" He helped the older woman step forward out of the pressing shoulders towering above her. "Peaches is in the first kennel on the right once we walk in."

He continued, pulling another woman into line behind Mary before the rest began sorting themselves out. Reassured their pets were safe, the emotions shifted from tense to anxious. Once everyone found a place, Trent pulled the keys from his pocket and nodded to Kara. Looking for all the world like a group of kindergarteners preparing for their first field trip, people shifted their feet, coughed, a few giggled.

Kara swiped a hand over her mouth. If he had to guess, she

was trying to wipe away a smile before it gave her away. Like with kindergarteners, any sign of weakness and they'd be doomed. He loved these people. Their ferocity, tenacity, and ability to love with deep tenderness gave them strength even as it made them slightly volatile.

"All right, everyone knows where to go?" Trent asked the question as he turned the key and pulled open the door.

People surged forward, but their general kindness and love for each other and the elderly couples in the front of the line kept everyone in check. No one wanted to be responsible for flattening their best friend's granny.

"Talk about showing up in the nick of time," Kara whispered at him as she passed.

"I do love being a hero."

Her chuckle thawed the ice from his veins. Seeing her vulnerable in that crowd had done something to his insides, shifted them, mutilated them...what exactly happened, he didn't know. Only that nothing wanted to go back to where it once was. A gap opened, revealing an empty spot aching to be filled.

As people lined the hall, the decibel rose amid a flurry of barks and squeals from several younger islanders. Clapping hands, excited shouts, the noise filled the building with more cheer than he'd ever heard.

These people, *his* people, loved with a fierceness and bravery that often hurt to experience. They'd suffered much, but here they stood, wiping tears and baby talking to their pets without shame.

It made his job worthwhile, seeing the bond between man and animal.

Kara hurried away, no doubt racing to the office where she could hide away with her camera. There'd be no time for pictures until the crowd disbursed. One couple ambled away, stopping to thank him and give assurances that they would be back to pick up their beagle within a week.

One man approached Trent and asked to take his dog home right away.

Kara reappeared, a stack of papers in her hand. She rushed toward Trent, already thumbing through the pages. Passing Trent a sheet with the man's name, ID, description, and which dog he owned—which Trent already knew—Kara paused and volleyed a look between them. "You're taking Ringo home today, correct?"

"Yes." Mr. Miller nodded and withdrew a matching slip of paper from his pocket. "Here's my release from the day I dropped him off. Things haven't been the same since then. I would have been by weeks ago, but my wife got sick, see, and we had to go to Atlanta for treatment." He blew his nose into a handkerchief, then shoved the mess back into his pocket. Thankfully, not the same pocket as where the paper had been.

"I understand. If you'll let Kara confirm the match, I'll get Ringo for you."

Mr. Miller shoved the paper Kara's way, while Trent returned the slip she'd handed him. Moving down the hall, he took a leash from the rack and approached Ringo's kennel. The elderly Basset Hound lounged near the door, his droopy eyes and overlong ears the only thing moving until Trent reached for the latch. Dragging himself up with a groan, his large paws shuffled forward. He waited with all the dignity of a gentleman for Trent to clip on the leash and give a soft "Let's go, boy" which drew the dog from the kennel and toward his waiting master.

The dog loped forward as fast as his old legs could move. Mr. Miller jogged to meet them, hunkering down to wrap his arms around his friend. Tears streamed down the weathered face. Tears Ringo washed away with a woof and swipe of his tongue. When Mr. Miller straightened, Ringo wagged his brown tail and strained toward the door to freedom.

Trent waved them on, holding back the surge of emotion

rolling up his own throat, while Kara wiped away tears and sniffled.

Another group approached, and they repeated the process, already synced into a rhythm as Kara anticipated his needs and acted before he knew what to do next.

By the time everyone left, five dogs had been returned to their homes. The ones left behind bayed, howled, and cried in disbelief as the owners walked away. Every eye held tears, some calling back their apologies and promising they'd return.

"They'll be okay." Trent reassured more than one heart-broken owner. "They'll still love you when you come back. Don't worry. They miss you, but I'll keep them safe and as happy as I can. You worry about getting things settled at home."

Hugs. Pats on the back. The occasional handshake. Each person attempted to show their gratitude. More than one offered him money, which he turned down.

The door closed behind the last person, and Trent sagged against the wall.

Kara shuffled the remaining papers into a neat stack and started to turn away.

"Thanks."

"For what?" She stopped, giving him a view of her profile. Tears had left streaks down her cheeks and her eyes puffy, but she'd never looked more beautiful. The love and compassion radiated from every nuance of her body language.

"You were great this morning. Out there and in here." He took a step toward her, then another, until they were face to face. "Johnson told you what happened? Warned you to be careful?"

Kara tucked her head against her shoulder. "He said Snake threatened you...and me."

"I didn't know if you'd come back to work. Wouldn't have blamed you if you didn't."

"He doesn't scare me."

"He should." Trent wrapped his fingers around her arm, keeping the touch soft as his thumb slid over the silky skin. His throat tightened at the idea of losing Kara. "But after seeing you take on that group this morning, I can see why one man wouldn't bother you." Even if the mention of Snake's threat dried Trent's mouth to dust.

"I didn't know what else to do. I couldn't let them frighten the animals. And they were scared. It was my fault they came. I should have made a clarification on the email and the flyer that their animals were not part of the adoption day festival."

"Word will spread now that they've been here. It'll turn right side up in no time." He motioned toward the office. "How are things going with the festival?"

"You won't believe who showed up at my house and helped organize everything."

Trent shoved all the feelings away and focused on Kara. The way her head tilted to the side as excitement spread her mouth into a wide smile. He needed her to feel safe, protected.

*B*y Friday night's meeting, Kara regretted every decision bringing her to this point. She entered the association building, arms loaded down with papers and knees knocking. *You can do this. Like the night with Mel.*

Her head knew, but her heart argued. She was not this person. Her idea of being part of a committee meant she obeyed orders, not stood in front of a crowd of eager men and women ready to take orders.

Her breath hiccupped, her stride faltering. *They're never going to listen to you.*

Mel appeared at Kara's side, smile beaming with friendship. "You can do this. We all believe in you. But if it's too much, we do understand." A frown twisted her expression into a grimace. "I know that sounds trite, being as I'm an extrovert and this seems easy to me, but I promise we won't bite." She patted Kara's arm and rushed away.

Dropping her papers onto a nearby chair, Kara waited for someone to take control. All around, people chatted and smiled. Occasionally someone glanced her way, then returned to their conversation.

Right. *She* was the one responsible for bringing this group to task. She cleared her throat and clasped her hands together behind her back to hide the shaking. "Could I have everyone's attention?" Her soft-spoken plea barely reached the first group.

One man nudged another, and the huddled group faced her.

Kara swallowed the nerves causing her voice to quiver and stepped toward the front of the room. "Excuse me? If everyone will take a seat, we'll get started."

In groups of twos and threes, the crowd slowly settled into the rows of chairs someone had placed. She made a mental note to find out who did that and thank them.

After the initial rush of chattering, Kara held up her hand. The room quieted. Her mouth developed a sudden need for moisture. Tongue thick and clinging to the roof of her mouth, she tried to speak, only to emit a tiny squeak. Her throat closed, her breath quickening until black spots dashed across her vision. Waving for Mel, Kara darted from the stage, running out into the cool night air where sweet relief sent chills down her spine.

"Kara?" Trent followed her around the barn, out of sight from the broad doors where Mel commanded the stage and the attention of every person.

"Go 'way." Hands on her knees, she pulled air into her starved lungs. Why, oh why, hadn't she asked someone else to be in charge tonight? Anyone could do a better job.

"I'm not going anywhere until I know you're okay."

His warm palm landed between her shoulder blades. The resulting gasp shot her upright, and his hand fell away. "I'm fine. Nerves." She shook out her hands and refused to look at him. To see the disappointment in his eyes. Disappointment she'd seen in her own mirror too many times after failing to overcome this fright attention brought with panicking waves.

"You're fine and I'm Muhammad Ali." Trent huffed, crossing his arms and leaning back against the wall. "You don't have to say what you think I want to hear, you know. I'm a big boy. I can handle the truth."

"And I don't need you to hold my hand and tell me everything's going to be all right. It's not okay. I can't do this. Put me behind a computer screen or a camera. But not this. I never should have tried."

"Okay."

Kara waited, anticipation boiling like acid. "Okay, what?"

"Don't lead the committee. I never meant for you to take on a role you didn't want. Let Mel organize and give orders. As long as it gets done." Trent lifted his head, and the soft shine of his eyes melted her already quivering knees. "You're more important."

Tears pricked. "Mel doesn't have time. I wanted to do this. To be someone people listen to. To be heard for once in my life."

"You *are* someone people listen to. You don't see it. And you don't have to force yourself to speak in front of a crowd to be heard."

A snuffle, covered by her hands brushing over her legs when she straightened to her full height didn't fool Trent. He took her chin between his thumb and forefinger, tilting her head to the light and ringing his hair with shadow. "God hears you, Kara. Even if no one else in this world ever heard a word you say, He does. And He loves you. Every part of you. None of this is a mistake. He created you, Kara, as you are, and He does not make mistakes."

"Then why can't I be brave? Why do my knees shake, and my hands sweat, and I feel like I'm going to puke when I'm in front of a crowd?"

"You might as well ask why the ocean is salty or the sky is blue. It is because God says it is. There's no one else on this earth like you. Others might have the same problems. In fact, I'm certain there are hundreds of thousands of people who feel the same as you. It's not a flaw." His thumb traced a short path across her chin, and his eyes followed the movement.

Kara let her breath slide out in a slow exhale, her hands itched to touch, to find the shape of his arms and hold on.

One second she was standing, debating the absurdity of reaching for Trent, the next, something warm and furry slammed into her legs, knocking her flat against his chest. She recognized the yips before Trent muttered the huskies' names, his breath fanning over her face with spicy cinnamon from the punch Mel had provided for tonight's event.

Trent's arms molded her body to his, the corded muscles twisting against her ribs.

After the speech he gave, he could kiss her now and she'd not stop him. Craved it, really, with an intensity her body had no idea what to do with.

When he lifted her away and lowered his hands, she took a shuddering breath.

"I should get them back home."

The "them" in question galloped around Trent's legs, sending dirt and sand flying every time they wheeled around.

"I could help." Kara waved toward where Mel's voice sent out the occasional trickle of sound. "They don't need me here."

"No. I'll go." Shoving the hair from his eyes, Trent frowned toward the darkness. "It's probably best if you're not around me too much. You heard what Johnson said. Snake's a threat. To you. To me. To anyone who crosses his path. I can't be responsible for something happening to you."

"You're not responsible for me. And especially not for Snake's actions. That's on him." Kara forced the needed intensity into her voice. "You're responsible for you, and only you."

"I wish I agreed with you." Trent whistled for the pups. "See you at work."

Kara let him disappear around the corner before her feet

followed. She crashed into the brush, catching up to the trio within a few strides.

"I told you not to come."

"No. You said it's probably best that I don't. I disagree. See. My actions. Not your responsibility."

"If you fall and break an ankle, I certainly will feel responsible."

Kara shrugged, but her heart did a little flip at the protective rumble in Trent's voice. "So I won't fall. Easy."

His silence answered her flippant response with a burst of heaviness. She wiggled her shoulders, urging the tension away. There was nothing wrong with helping Trent take the pups home. The dark night had no power to reach out and hold her captive. Hopper Island was about as safe a place as a person could find. Snake aside, the darkness pressing around them trembled with peace. Gentle breezes ruffled the loblolly pines, sending the scent of pine to bite through the salty tang of the air.

Their footsteps fell in tandem across the parking lot, with the occasional yip and scuffle of paws as the dogs raced in ever-widening circles. Trent whistled again, a short order that called the pups back to his side with waving tails and joy-filled eyes.

"Do you plan on keeping them?"

"No."

"Why not? They obviously love you."

"I have a rule about adopting. Foster but never adopt."

Kara peered through the dark, taking in the hard line of his jaw and straight shoulders. His steps changed from easy glide to stomps before he stopped by the truck. "Seems you don't care for your own rule."

"It's not that…" He rubbed both palms over his face, letting out a frustrated sound somewhere between a growl and a scoff. "If I adopt one, I'll be tempted to adopt them all. And we know that's impossible. They deserve a good home, with families who'll shower them with affection, take them for walks, and spend days at the beach. I live in a shoebox and spend most of my time at work. There's no room for anything else in my life."

The words carved out her heart while it still beat. All those moments. The near kisses and smoldering looks straight from the novels. They'd all meant nothing? Or did he mean anything only in regards to animals? The word choice meant something. Didn't it? Anything...not any*one*.

"Who do you think you owe?"

Trent dug his hands through his hair, his feet rooted to the ground even as his torso swiveled to face her. "I don't know what you're talking about."

"Oh, but you do." Kara poked her finger into his chest. "You live in a shoebox because you choose to. But you built one of the most impressive obstacle courses I've ever seen. Which means you have money and options. Your truck barely runs, but you buy me a new camera because you feel guilty for losing mine. I might be a shy, quiet, introvert, but I see things. I notice people. And you're trying to make up for something."

She helped herself to Trent's passenger seat and slammed the door despite her trembling hands. If he thought he'd get rid of her that easily, he'd not learned nearly enough these last few weeks.

15

*T*rent tasted Kara's words during the drive home. While the dream of restitution tasted sweet, the reality soured. Of course, he needed to make up for his past. Why didn't she understand that? *Because she doesn't* know *your past. You never told her.*

A deep sigh, drowned out by the truck's rattling cough, pressed against Trent's lips. He shook his head and left the truck, motioning for the dogs to jump from the back.

Kara met him at the tailgate, a soft breeze tugging her skirt toward the shadows cast by the crescent moon.

"Look, Kara—" A sharp yip, followed by a menacing growl, pulled Trent toward the house.

A man's shout and the yelp of a pup pushed his legs to pound faster. He broke through the foliage, chest heaving to compensate for the mad sprint, and slid to a stunned halt.

Red graffiti covered his front door and bled a slow death across the house, the artist interrupted, leaving a half-completed tag. But enough of the mark had been completed for Trent to understand the intent. He followed the letters, his mind churning them over and over T-R-A-I-…

Kara called out for the dogs, her voice stopping Trent as he took a step forward. Whoever did this—and he only needed one guess to figure that out—might still be around, waiting for a chance to increase the damage counter. One threat to Kara was one too many. Putting her in the direct path of this? Unthinkable.

"You should go." Trent turned, casting the words over his shoulder.

Phone pressed to her ear, Kara wrinkled her nose before she turned away. "Yes. Trent Raines' home has been vandalized. No. We haven't gone inside. We interrupted whoever was here. Yes. We'll wait." Kara palmed the phone and faced him again. "You were saying?"

"I said you should go. It might not be safe."

"So...you want me to leave you here...alone. In a place you think might not be safe. Um. Yeah. That's a big, fat no from me." Kara crossed her arms and cocked a hip, a perfect image of defiance.

How did she go from a puddling mess when faced with a crowd to this knotted ball of courage when face-to-face with danger? He didn't understand it, or her. He wanted her safely out of the way. Opening his mouth to say exactly that, he remembered the cry of pain from one of the pups. "Remus. Romulus. Come."

Their answering howls sounded from behind the house, and he started forward. Kara snagged his sleeve, pulling him back. "We're not supposed to get any closer. There might be evidence. Footprints or something. If we go tromping around, it'll mess things up."

"They might be hurt." Trent eased his arm away, not wanting to hurt Kara by giving in to the fury beginning to burn through his veins and light fire to his muscles, demanding action.

Kara let him slide away a single step before her head tilted, and she gave him a look he'd come to love. That open, innocent expression burrowed deep inside, reflecting a sliver of light into the dark spaces.

Remus came loping around the side of the house, tongue hanging from his mouth. Romulus tagged along at his brother's heels, a slight limp holding him back from a full-on run. The pups flopped to the ground at his feet.

"Should I call Kendall?" Kara wiggled her phone.

Their resident mobile vet would be happy to make a late afternoon call, but Trent motioned for Kara to wait. "Let me look him over. It might be a thorn or something." Running his hands over the pup, he found nothing that might be broken. No gashes. No blood, and nothing in the dog's paw that indicated trouble. Trent conceded defeat at the same moment the flash of headlights brightened the gruesome display of red paint tainting his home. "Call Kendall. I'll see who's here."

Deputy Johnson hitched up his sagging board shorts and shrugged into a frayed t-shirt while walking toward Trent. "You missed some great waves today." The joviality dropped from his voice when he saw the damage inflicted on the off-white paint. He whistled. "You've ticked someone off. I'm guessing we both know who."

"Has to be Snake. That's his mark." Trent pointed toward the "I" splashed in vivid red. "See the shape of the lettering? Looks like a snake's fang. That's his tag. Always has been."

"That might be enough to bring him in for questioning, but anyone who knows could have made that tag. Unless we get concrete proof, he'll slide right out of the charges."

"As usual." Trent ran his hand over his head and down the back of his neck. "First threats against Kara, now this. He has to be stopped, Christian."

"We'll get him." Christian slapped a hand against Trent's shoulder with enough force to send a sharp sting across his skin. "Now, let me check things out, then you can go inside and see if anything's missing. Go check on your girl. I'll be right back."

Trent trudged back to Kara, Christian's words not completely sinking in until he stopped by her side and hunkered down. *Your girl.* Their hands brushed over Romulus's coat, coming closer together with each swipe. The pup rolled onto his back and stuck all four paws into the air, begging for a belly rub. Trent's chuckle matched Kara's.

"Kendall's on her way."

Trent let gravity carry him back until he sat on the cold ground. Why did everything have to come apart at the seams? Why now? He didn't like it. His skin itched with the need to do something. To fix the problems, force them away, and right the world onto the axis where his actions now made up for his past mistakes.

"When I was eighteen, I broke into Christian's house then left the Islands after his dad forced me to work all summer to repay the damages. Spent the next year in the city. Met up with Snake and joined his crew. Living as a pastor's kid, I had a great life. More privilege than I deserved and no idea of what I'd be giving up when I ventured out on my own. I wanted excitement. Adventure. And I didn't think I'd find that here." Hands laced together over his knees, Trent kept his attention on Romulus, who'd decided to wiggle closer to Kara's stroking hand.

Remus nosed her side, sending her toppling forward. Trent caught her before the ground could. She stared up at him, eyes wide and curious but free of condemnation or distrust. With a "then what" look, she settled by his side and took one of his hands into hers. His chilled fingers warmed at the embrace.

"It was fun, at first. Parties all the time. No rules. I could have anything I wanted, and no one to tell me no. The first time he took me to a dogfight, I was appalled. Then he showed me the money. Convinced me that when you found the right dogs, the ones that enjoyed fighting, that made it okay." Trent stopped, took a good look at the defaced home, the results of his actions finally catching up, and shook his head.

"I made it okay in my head. Started training dogs to fight. To win. Then, one day, one turned on me. Not his fault. I'd taught him to be that way. And I paid the price for it. We both did." His fingers found the scar wrapping around his forearm, and Kara's were already there, tracing the lines, the ragged edges, and deep grooves.

Johnson waved at Trent from the front door. "All clear out here. Let's check the inside."

Kara stood first, her fingers still linked with his. As she stared back at him, the fierceness he'd come to recognize blazed out, warming the cold center of his heart. "And still, after admitting you paid for your actions, you continue to do this to yourself. You don't deserve it, Trent. You're so much more than the sum of your mistakes."

Her faith made him want to move mountains to prove Kara right. To prove he'd earned the right to be part of something again instead of trying to shove together the broken pieces of his mistakes until they made something worthwhile.

Rolling her words around as they walked, Trent squeezed her fingers. She returned the gesture and wrapped her free hand around his arm, linking them together. His hand brushed her leg with every step, the touch intoxicating in a way he'd never experienced.

Fishing the key from his pocket, Trent handed it over to Christian and stepped back, letting the other man lead the way. The fact the lock remained intact gave a feeling of security. Perhaps they had interrupted Snake before he'd done more than tag the house.

Christian stepped across the threshold, and his low whistle sent Trent's stomach dropping through the floor. "There's no need for you to come inside right now. Let me check things out first. Then you can tell me if anything is missing or destroyed."

Kara squeezed his arm, the press of her fingers the only thing he could feel aside from the boiling rage and disappointment. "This isn't your fault. His actions. His responsibility. Remember?"

Oh, he remembered all right. If he'd never gone to the mainland, none of this would be happening.

16

*S*aturday morning's golden light strained across the island. Standing with her back to the water and her camera pointed at Hopper's lighthouse, Kara adjusted the ISO and took another test shot. A frustrated sigh escaped at the mottled black encroaching along the edges of the photo.

"Trouble in paradise?"

A delighted shiver took the place of her frustrated breath. After leaving his house last night, she hadn't been sure if Trent would ever care to see her again. Yet, here he stood, braced against the onslaught of wind and surf with his hands tucked behind his back and a little boy gleam in his baby blues.

A hundred thoughts flashed through her mind, but she held them all back, each one discarded as sounding harsh or dismissive. *Didn't expect to see you today. Thought you'd be at the shelter today.* Kara chomped the piece of gum she'd already mangled and worked her face into an expression she hoped showed her joy at his sudden appearance.

"Cat got your tongue?" Another question, and a step closer. Trent's expression started to fall.

"After what I said last night, I feared you might never want to see me again." *No! You weren't supposed to say that. What are you thinking?* She fiddled with the camera strap chafing her neck and glanced back at the lighthouse. The perfect shot hovered there, in the golden hour of sunrise, but her old, clunky camera didn't have the ability to capture the image stamped across her mind.

"You mean, after you told me I'm not responsible for everyone else's actions. Only my own." Trent took another step, hands still behind his back. "You know...my dad's been telling me the same thing for years, and I couldn't grasp it. Felt like he was placating me, you know? It's what parents do. They make their kids feel better."

"He's not wrong, and he didn't say it to ease your guilty conscience." Camera to her eye, Kara clicked the shutter, praying the image magically transported itself to the display screen. If anything, the second shot proved worse than the first.

"Here." Trent laughed when she growled and shook the camera. Taking the behemoth from her hands, he lifted it from her neck and passed her a square red and white box with Canon written across the lid. "Try this."

She scanned the box, tilting it one way- then another as the specs fired her synapses into overdrive. "This—It's not—" She pulled open the lid and almost shrieked. "This isn't the camera I showed you. Please tell me I didn't ask for this."

"You didn't ask for this." Trent beamed, the hand-caught-in-the-cookie-jar grin morphing into full got-you laughter. "After you left the office that day, I did some research. You asked for a camera that was new three years ago. This seemed better."

"Better? Better! Are you kidding me? It's like comparing a hot air balloon to the Hindenburg." Kara caressed the sleek casing, memorizing the weight and placement of her most used buttons. "I can't wait to try it out."

"Good thing I charged it for you." Trent motioned to where she'd left her backpack. "Extra batteries and goodies are there, by your bag. Everything else you need is in the box." He shuffled his feet in the sand and shoved his free hand into the pockets of his shorts. "I wanted to give it to you so you could practice. I heard you're shooting Mel and Zeke's wedding next weekend." Turning, he lost the bit of excitement that for a moment had lifted his shoulders and tugged his mouth out of its perpetual frown.

"Don't go." She shot the words after him, her arm stretching out to stop him. "If you have time, I mean. I could use your help testing out the new camera. I shouldn't keep it. But I'm going to. Consider it a business investment since the majority of use will come from the shelter."

"It's a gift. You don't owe me anything in return."

"No, but it will benefit the shelter, too. Even you can admit that my work the last few weeks has been sub-par thanks to that old thing." She motioned to the camera still in his hand before nodding her head toward the lighthouse. "Come on. If you're not doing anything else today, I need to practice shooting people."

"If the wrong person heard you right now, they'd have Christian down here investigating." Fiddling with the buttons on the camera, he lifted it to his eye. "How do you even know what all this stuff does?"

"Practice. Now, come on." She snagged his sleeve and pulled him toward the towering structure. "Walk toward the lighthouse while I fix the settings. I want to practice some action shots. Can't very well ask them to stop the wedding while I get the perfect shot."

With a shake of his head, Trent strode away. Kara spent a moment admiring the muscles bunching with each step before shaking off the flutters of attraction and focusing on her new baby. A knob twist here, raise the ISO there, a rapid-fire test shot, check the display. Adjust the aperture, and by the time Trent reached the last rise, she had everything perfect. Framing him to the right, using the rule of thirds, she angled toward the light, letting it cast Trent in shadow.

A quick press on the shutter and she had a three-shot line up of almost identical images, each one crisp and clean.

She started to call him to walk back toward her, maybe even convince him to run—for the sake of practice—when he waved for her to join him. His urgent shushing motion while ducking into a stand of shrubs sent Kara scurrying toward him.

"Nigel and Darcy," he hissed in her ear when she fell to the sand beside him. "I think he's going to propose. You should take pictures."

"I can't take pictures without their permission!"

"Shhhhh. I'm giving you permission. Believe me, Darcy will want them. You're going to miss it. Hurry." His arm wrapped around her waist and hauled her close while he pointed through a tiny opening in the shrub. "Right there."

Kara wriggled deeper into the sand and lifted the camera to her eye. Keeping the other eye open, she watched for anything approaching that might interfere with the shot.

Hand in hand, Nigel and Darcy strolled the beach, looking for all the world like a couple perfectly in love. The adoration and love on Nigel's face made Kara's own heart ache. Oh, to feel that amount of love focused on her. To know someone loved her with the love afforded within God's perfect love.

Ocean surf washed the words away, but Kara didn't need a script when Nigel dropped to one knee in front of the lighthouse and ripped a blue box from his pocket.

Click.

Darcy's squeal and hands slapping over her mouth.

Click.

The smile so wide it had to pinch Nigel's cheeks.

Click.

Kara documented every second from the shifting expressions to the ring sliding over Darcy's finger and Nigel scooping her into his arms and whirling them both in a circle. That one was her favorite. With Nigel's blatant love on display and Darcy's arms around his neck as she threw her head back and laughed. That moment encompassed everything Kara knew about their relationship. Best friends first. And now they would cement that bond in holy matrimony.

She continued clicking until the couple walked out of sight, only then feeling the wetness on her cheeks. Trent pulled a bandana from his pocket, eyebrow lifting as he moved to wipe her face. With her hands full of camera, Kara allowed his actions and tried not to let the shroud of embarrassment cloud the perfect moment.

When Trent scuffed his shoulder against his own eyes, she risked a closer look. Tears hovered on his lashes, dashed away by his quick motions but undeniable. "Must be something in the air around here. Mel and Zeke. Now Darcy and Nigel."

The gruff tone argued with the tender expression as he swiped his thumb over her cheek and returned the bandana to his pocket.

"Whatever it is, I'll take a dose." She stared at a spot over Trent's shoulder, not wanting to meet his eyes after the admission for fear he'd see her as foolish. Or worse, begging for a relationship he didn't want.

"Marriage seems like a fine way to spend a life."

Kara settled deeper into the sand and turned the camera display his direction where Darcy's love for Nigel shone straight through the glass. "Love like that? Absolutely."

17

*S*unday morning, after a rather focused sermon on the prodigal son, Trent wandered once again to his childhood home. Standing on the front porch, his fist hovered at the door. With a deep breath and squaring his shoulders, he pulled the screen door open and stepped inside.

"Dad?"

"Kitchen." The answering reply held no trace of surprise, only the reliable depth and acceptance his dad afforded anyone who crossed his threshold. Emerging from the kitchen with a plate in one hand and a glass of tea in the other, his dad's face split into a wide smile. "Trent! Didn't expect to see you today."

"You know someone else who calls you Dad?" The idea burned deep and scorching. Another son who wouldn't put the man he admired through so much grief probably would be welcome.

"Nah." Saluting him with the glass, he took a long drink.

"You let anyone walk in your front door and tell them where you are?" Trent crossed his arms in mock annoyance. "What if I was a burglar?" The same argument they'd volleyed back and forth over the years landed in his father's court with a thud.

"Then you'd be meeting the poorest rich man on Hopper." The cackle rattled a little more in these recent years, but the spark still lit his eyes. "See something you want? You're welcome to take it. Can't go with me when I die, might as well let someone else enjoy it." He harrumphed and dropped into his recliner, carefully balancing the plate on his knee. "Lunch is in the kitchen. Help yourself. Chicken salad and sweet tea."

Trent followed the unspoken order and arranged a plate of sandwiches onto the old china plate, a relic from his parents' honeymoon. A quick prayer, and Trent shoved half the sandwich in his mouth. Maybe it would fortify him for the conversation he knew they needed to have but he'd been avoiding for years.

"Spit it out before you choke on it."

He didn't mean the sandwich.

Pastor Dad to the heart of the matter. Or as close as he could get with what little information he had.

"Did you get angry when Mom died?"

"Now that's a question I didn't expect." Squinted eyes hardened into blue chips of ice. His dad lowered the sandwich and brushed his hands together, knocking crumbs onto the plate. "Every day."

Trent couldn't speak. The words stuck in his throat, as large and bulky as any boulder. Not once in his life had his dad shown anger.

Setting the plate aside before folding his hands over his stomach, his dad closed his eyes a beat longer than a blink. When they opened, tears fled the corners and tracked a line of wrinkles down his weathered cheeks. "I did my best to hide it from you. I wonder now if I did too good a job. You didn't seem to know how to grieve, and seeing me lose my temper might have pushed you over the edge. You had enough anger for both of us."

"I never knew."

"You never caught me the nights I snuck out to the beach and screamed, shouting at God and asking Him why He took her from us. Or the days when I couldn't breathe for the pain ripping me apart." Lips trembling, tears now rolling in fat drops, his dad leaned forward and locked eyes with Trent. "There were days when I even grew angry with your mother."

His confusion must have been strewn across his face, because a wave of compassion dropped over his dad's countenance.

"Grief is a personal battle, son. Some people handle it better than others. The only person I was never angry at was you."

"I blamed her, too." Trent's head sagged forward, his chin landing in his palm while he anchored the weight on the chair's arm. "I believed she wanted to leave us. If she'd really loved us, she would have fought harder. It wasn't fair of me, but I couldn't help it."

"Death is never fair to those it leaves behind." Remorse lowered the raspy voice to a whisper. "And even though I know she's in a better place, I catch myself wishing she were still here with us. As selfish as that would be, I wanted to live this life together for many more years."

"And then I ran away, leaving you to grieve again."

"But you came home."

"And brought all my troubles back with me." Trent massaged his temples, the headache morphing into a throbbing beat. "My old life is catching up, and I don't know how to hold back the tide of repercussions. The waves are drowning me."

"Stop trying to hold them back on your own. God's got this, Trent. Stop jumping in front of Him. Let Him carry you. He's the master of the waves, and only He can turn back the tide. He may choose to let this battle be one you must fight, but He will fight it alongside you. You've never been alone. Even when you left here, you took God with you." The work-roughed hands clenched and released, the urgency reddening his father's fingers. "Whatever you're facing, stand *with* God and face it together."

He rolled the words around, letting them ease the turmoil. Stand with God. Had he not been? Trent backtracked through the past months. Nothing had changed in his routine. Morning Bible studies. Church on Sunday and Wednesday. Prayers every day. But had he ever asked God to help with the situation where Snake had taken hold of Trent's life?

No.

The answer rattled him, sending out shockwaves of regret. Years of knowledge, of being a Christian, and he'd lost his way during the first major obstacle thrown in his path. A hurricane that tossed the island found a way into his heart as well, ripping up his carefully cultivated power lines—his connection to God.

"I've been an idiot."

"No, son. You've been relying on self. It's an easy trap to fall into. And one that can take a major catastrophe to get us out of the hole we've dug." He patted Trent's knee before leaning back in the recliner. "Now. Tell me what's blown you off course, and then we'll pray about it."

Trent leaned into the plush upholstery and explained everything that had occurred. Leaving nothing out, from Snake's appearance to his mixed emotions over Kara, Trent spilled his emotional upheaval across the floor.

Upon concluding the last few weeks of trouble, his dad frowned but nodded his head. "Do you remember the day you came back?"

He doubted his dad referred to the previous Sunday, but instead meant to call him back to the day many years ago when Trent plodded up the sandy tract with nothing but a mangled arm and a repentant heart.

At his nod, his dad leaned forward, expression intent. "And you remember the look on my face?"

Trent shook his head, trying in vain to recall anything about that day other than the miserable failure he'd become and his desire to crawl beneath the largest boulder and never climb out. Then, between one breath and the next, an image flashed. His dad, stepping out onto that rickety porch, with his arms held wide and the broadest, most innocent smile on his weathered face. A look so tender and welcoming, he didn't know how he'd ever forgotten the warmth that spread through him when he realized his dad welcomed him home.

He'd stepped into that embrace, completely broken and undeserving, and received the sweetest words ever spoken. "My son, welcome home."

"You showed me love, even then."

"Especially then." His dad corrected with a smile and pat on Trent's knee. "The world had chewed you up and spit you out. The last thing you needed was me adding coals to an already blazing bout of guilt."

"You're saying I should welcome Snake?" Trent wagged his head and shoved his hands between his knees to stop them from clenching into fists. "I don't think that's a good idea."

"No. You misunderstand. Snake believes you've betrayed him. Abandoned him and the 'family' he provided for you. Misguided though he is, Snake showed you the only compassion he knew how."

"And I should show him the same grace you extended to me." It made sense, in an odd, incomprehensible sort of way. They'd been something of a family during his time in the city. The day Trent walked away without a goodbye was as much a slap in Snake's face as it had been to his dad. After all the instruction and careful tutoring, he'd thrown it in both men's faces without thought for what they'd given up for him.

Young punk that he'd been, taking responsibility for the rash actions landing him in constant trouble never occurred to him. Now, looking back, with the hindsight of an adult and the wisdom pressed upon him through the years, his abandoning of others tacked on yet another irresponsible action. Another problem he could never take back but one that had followed him, growing more rancid with each passing year.

ara plodded through another work week with all the fervor of anticipating a tooth extraction. With the exception of seeing Trent every day, and working alongside him, the entire week created zero excitement.

But Saturday rolled around again. Mel and Zeke's wedding, and excitement kept her up too late into the night. Eyeing herself in the mirror, Kara frowned and patted concealer over the dark shadows under her eyes.

After making the final touches of blush and a swipe of lip gloss, she tossed her backpack over one shoulder, then had to smooth the sleeves of her soft pink dress before sliding her feet into matching heels.

Even if she'd rather spend her days in leggings, the chance to dress up in something feminine and flattering drew her with a ferocious gnawing.

"They won't even know you're there." Kara reassured herself in the hall mirror while checking that the curls she'd spent hours on remained loose yet orderly instead of wild and uncouth. "Photographers are there to see everyone else. Not the other way around." The thought of photographing moments like she'd captured between Darcy and Nigel made her blood pound and a smile bloom without contention. "Be polite. Compliment the dresses."

She checked the backpack. Darcy and Nigel's photos nestled snug in a protected sleeve, safe from scratches or creases. They begged to see the light one last time before she passed them along to the happily engaged couple. Images that had seared themselves into her memories and teased her dreams with ideas of happily ever after and soul mates.

Drawing courage from the weight of her camera pressing across one shoulder, Kara swung open the front door and leaped back, upsetting her balance on the rarely worn heels.

Trent jumped, catching her around the waist before she landed flat on her back like an upside-down turtle.

"My camera!" Swiveling her head, Kara searched for the canvas bag.

Trent hauled her back to her feet, his chuckle bright as the morning sunrise tracking across her floor. "You nearly break yourself and you're worried about that camera." After steadying her, he patted the strap still secured over her shoulder. "Your camera's fine."

"I'd hate to think what would happen if you caused me to lose another one."

"Me? How'd it be my fault?"

"You scared the dickens outta me! What are you doing here, anyway?" Hand on hip, she strummed her fingertips in a steady staccato.

"Taking you to the wedding?" His voice lifted on the last word, making it a question. An especially cute question to match the charm oozing from his dressed-up persona of wedding casual.

White shirt, ironed and crisp against his tanned skin. Black dress pants and what had to be the shiniest pair of dress shoes across the Independence Islands. Even his curls had been tamed.

Kara imagined that took some heavy-duty gel and a lot more patience than she'd given him credit for.

She whistled, waving her hand to indicate the dress clothes. "Nice get up. But I don't remember agreeing to go with you. I'm on my way there now to take pre-wedding shots, and I'll be there later than everyone else to wrap up."

"I know. Mel told me. That's how I knew to come now instead of later."

"Mel asked you to bring me?"

"No." Trent rubbed his palms together, and she'd swear a blush crept up his neck. "I mentioned that I'd not asked anyone to come with me. Mel mentioned you'd not RSVP'd a guest. So I came by in the hopes you would let me drive you over and, well, I didn't think beyond that. What'd'ya say? Be my date?"

Talk about a heart skipping a beat. Kara's flash of temper melted away quicker than snow on a tropical island. Something she'd experience for herself if Trent managed to complete her wish list of ideas for the adoption day festival. Not that she'd hold her breath in anticipation. No sense fainting like one of those goats she'd seen on the funniest pet videos.

Trent waited, his hands doing that tapping thing over the scar and his expression growing more uncertain. Once again, she'd left him wondering while her thoughts ran a hundred different directions.

"Yeah. Okay. You know I'm working though, right? Being my date will be like not having a date at all. Mel's counting on me to document her wedding. I can't let her down."

"You won't." Trent beamed and held the door. "And you won't hear a peep from me that you'd rather spend all your time behind your camera instead of dancing with me."

"I won't hear it, huh. Not a word."

"My lips are sealed." He mimed the old zippered-lips action.

Too bad, because those lips were meant to be kissed. Often.

Kara shifted her shoulders, willing the stray thoughts to fall away. They clung tighter, holding on better than Granny's false teeth during a caramel apple eating contest. The absolute last thing she needed to be thinking about during a wedding was Trent's lips.

When did December on Hopper turn into a second wave of summer? Kara fanned her hand around her face, hoping to push back the scalding temperature. No doubt, her cheeks had turned red enough to fry eggs.

"Everything okay?"

"Yep!" Her voice cracked worse than a teenage boy's, sending another flare of heat raging across her cheeks. "We should go. I can't be late."

"Right." Trent scanned her face, eyebrows scooting closer together as he inspected her. "You're the boss." He helped boost her into the truck, then hurried around to the driver's side while she tucked the backpack between her feet.

"Talk about déjà vu." Shaking his head, Trent motioned toward her and the bag. "Good thing we're heading over to Merriweather or this would be too weird."

"For your lips to be sealed, you talk an awful lot."

His laughter exploded outward, shoulders shaking and eyes pressed tight, he cranked the engine. "You're feistier than I gave you credit for."

"Yeah, well, get to know me a little more and you'll see what I've really been hiding."

"Can't wait."

He made it sound like a promise.

By the time they arrived at the wedding venue, which ended up being Zeke's grandmother's house, Kara's fidgeting had ended with Trent drawing her hand across the seat to rest inside his palm. With thoughtful—albeit quick—glances and words of encouragement, he eased the fear crawling around her insides.

Each argument of good Kara versus evil Kara ended with good Kara winning.

You're not good enough to shoot a wedding. Ping! Evil Kara took a jab.

Remember Nigel and Darcy. Those pictures were perfect. Score for good Kara.

Trent's thumb grazed her knuckle before he gave her hand a squeeze and let go. The engine rumbled, then grew silent, leaving her with a tightness in her throat at the enormity of the task looming ahead.

"Stop." Trent settled his hands on her shoulders. "You're freaking out. Tell me why. What's the worst thing that could happen?"

"I'll ruin the wedding."

"How?"

"My pictures won't be good enough."

"What happens if that's true? What if your pictures aren't good enough?"

"Mel will hate me, and I'll never be able to take pictures again."

"Have you ever known Mel to hate anyone?"

"No. But I don't know her as well as you." Her breathing accelerated, the gasps coming faster.

Trent squeezed, his fingers sending pings of heat to counter the sudden cold spreading through her limbs. "One: Mel has never hated anyone. I don't think she's capable. Two: You're a wonderful photographer. Trust yourself. Say a prayer, pull yourself together, remember all those hours of classes and the years you've spent working toward this moment. And that's not helping because now you're breathing like a locomotive." He squeezed again. "You can do this, Kara. I believe in you. So does Mel." He winked. "Even if you're the biggest failure ever as a wedding photographer, you'll still be number one in my book."

"I'm not sure if I should kiss you, or push you down in the nearest mudhole."

"The first one sounds pretty good to me."

And before she could open her mouth to protest, his lips covered hers.

What had she been worried about?

Trent's hands slid over her shoulders and up to cup her neck.

She molded her fingers to the shape of his sides, the starched cotton soft on her fingertips in contrast to the ribs beneath. Her head swam with the feel of his lips, the heat shifting from flicker to inferno between one breath and the next.

When he leaned away, the sheer weight of her eyelids left her speechless.

"Are you going to do that every time I spaz out?"

"I'd love to." The husky timbre drew her eyes open, curious to see if he'd been as affected by their kiss. Eyes half-closed, he slid his hands down her arms and cupped her elbows.

Intoxicated by the half-lidded gaze, Kara shifted closer and shivered when his thumbs grazed the back of her arms. She needed to leave. Trent squeezed her arms, his breathing as ragged as her own. Her toe bumped against canvas, the scrape of sound breaking through thoughts of a second kiss.

1 9

*E*yes only half open, Trent brushed his thumbs along the edge of Kara's sleeves. Warning bells rang in tune with her shiver. Not a single date and he'd kissed the girl. There should be a country song about the repercussions of those types of actions.

Kara shifted toward her door, her eyes still holding a glaze of being properly kissed and no longer afraid of the mission looming overhead. She started to speak, a blush creeping along her cheeks. Instead, she gave her head a minuscule shake and retreated.

Trent tugged his collar and let the breeze cool a strip of skin as he slid from the truck and followed Kara toward the front door.

Hand lifted to knock, Kara cocked her head in his direction. "No distractions."

"On my honor." He held up a pinky, intending to link their fingers together in a childhood show of promise. Kara hooked her pinky through his. When she started to pull away, he held tighter, that small pressure of skin enough to hold him anchored in her presence.

"Well, don't stand out there looking all googly-eyed at each other. Come inside where I can see you." Miss Evelyn bumped the door open and waved both hands. "Come on. Don't let the dog out. Last thing we need is another of Daphne's escapes." She pursed her lips, a thoughtful expression on her aged face. "Then again, you two look like you could use an island dog hunt yourselves."

Kara flushed brighter and pulled her pinky from his. "I'm here to take pictures. Can you direct me to Mel's room? She wanted pre-wedding shots of her and the bridesmaids."

With a mild huff that said Miss Evelyn wouldn't be thwarted for long, she motioned toward the staircase arching overhead. "Up the steps, first door on the right. Men are down the hall on the left. Best knock before you go in there." She winked and jabbed a finger in Trent's direction. "Or send that one in to scope out the place for you."

Dropping his hand to the small of Kara's back, Trent paced himself to her shorter stride. The heels lifted Kara enough to put them at eye level, but since she kept ducking her head, he'd not been able to take advantage of the new height variant. "I'll be waiting for you out here." His hand hovered, and he drew it back, letting his fingertips trail across the narrow space before lowering himself to a nearby bench covered in red velvet.

Kara disappeared into the room as a wash of feminine laughter burst from the open door. She gave him one last smile, the widening of her eyes revealing the return of fear.

He winked, a slow, lazy movement, promising he'd make good on his earlier statement if she allowed it.

Down the hall, male voices rose and fell in tandem. Zeke stepped from another room, adjusting a navy vest and twisting his head from side to side. Catching sight of Trent, Zeke beamed a smile bright enough to blind and jerked Trent into a hug. Where he'd once considered Trent competition for Mel's affections, Zeke's back-slapping embrace spoke of brotherhood.

After releasing Trent, Zeke took a breath and reached up to swipe his hand through his hair. Stopping halfway, he grimaced. "You're here early."

"I brought Kara. She's taking pictures of Mel. Of the wedding, I should say." Trent shrugged and his gaze tugged its way back to the door. "Is there anything I can do to help?"

"Honestly"—Zeke looked around with a hint of panic—"I have no idea what's going on. I know where I'm supposed to be in half an hour and that's it. So if you want to join the rest of the guys while we waste time, feel free. I'm heading down to grab something to drink."

"Better not spill something on that tux. Mel'll have your skin."

Zeke ran his hands over the silk vest, a wry grin twisting his mouth. "Maybe I'll wait till after the wedding. Just in case." He backed down the hall, his own attention riveted on the closed door where his bride-to-be waited. "I've never known a day to go this slow."

Trent agreed. His intention had been to spend the day with Kara once he figured out how to work around her photography. And after their kiss in his truck, Kara's attention climbed a few notches on his scale.

The half hour passed, but as Zeke said, it crept by slower than filling an hourglass one grain of sand at a time.

When Kara emerged and hurried down the hall, Trent followed, taking up residence behind her. Far enough away she could move without bumping him but close enough the scent of her shampoo lingered with every breath.

She captured pictures of everything. From the centerpieces on the array of tables to the cake standing in the middle of the pavilion Zeke built last year, Kara shot from every angle imaginable and some he'd never have considered.

Seemingly satisfied, she found a spot along the wall and positioned the camera on a tripod. Having never been inside

Miss Evelyn's home before, Trent had nothing to compare the room to, but the drapes of white material contrasted well with the rich wood tones.

"Bet you're glad to have a digital camera instead of working with film." His attempt at breaking the ice fell flat when Kara shot him a look that appeared partially disgusted yet frantic.

"No distractions. Remember. This is important to me."

"And you're important to *me*. You have time to take a breath. You're doing great." Trent slid his hand along her arm and gave a reassuring squeeze.

"This is the most important part. The ceremony. Mel and Zeke need these pictures to be perfect. I can't mess up." She hardened her jaw, sparks igniting in her eyes. "I won't mess up. I can do this."

Trent nodded. "That's my girl."

Kara let the comment slide.

He'd take that as a win.

A woman took a seat at the grand piano, flipped open a book, and set her fingers to the ivory keys. As the music began to swell and couples filled the seats, Kara stood motionless, her attention locked on the camera. Trent listened to the occasional click of the shutter. Kara pressed against his side when she swiveled, lining up the camera with the entryway where Mel would make her appearance.

The music changed again, the wedding march drifting lazily through the room. Mel entered, her arm looped through her dad's and a brilliant smile on her face. Kara clicked, and Mel walked.

Trent stared. Not at Mel as everyone else did, although she was beautiful, but at Kara, whose winsome smile had shifted as she wiped away a tear and continued to press the shutter button.

He dragged his attention to the bride, catching the oohs and aahs of the crowd when her gown glittered from a dusting of sequins, beads, and baubles. The off the shoulder cut suited her, as did the fitted waist and five-foot-long train trailing behind.

What dress would Kara pick for her wedding day? And why did that thought send his hand tugging at his collar?

By will alone, Trent made it through the ceremony without staring again at Kara. He hoped. He took in everything else, from the dopey smile on Zeke's face to the chandelier casting minute shadows over the guests.

Miss Evelyn had allowed her home to be transformed, bringing the flash of romance to mix with the melody of beach and waves in her staid home.

Mel's bridesmaids—dressed in some sort of baby blue confection he couldn't begin to name—pressed hands to their hearts when Zeke dipped Mel for their first kiss as a married couple.

Kara hiccupped a breath, never letting go of the camera.

If she'd not taken a thousand pictures, he'd eat his belt.

Mel laughed, bringing Trent back.

Zeke held her arm, pulling her down the aisle and out into the yard where refreshments waited.

Kara hurried behind, camera bundled in her arms while the backpack banged her hip.

Trent moved to take something from her, only to be pushed away with a grunt. The bobbling camera called for Kara's complete concentration. No doubt his attempt to help had been more of a hindrance.

With everyone now outside, Kara removed the tripod and slipped through the crowd. Pointing the camera in every direction, she clicked, shifted, clicked.

A grin teased him when Kara tossed her heels aside, sat down on the ground, and pointed the camera up toward Mel and Zeke. Pink leggings flashed beneath the skirt. Popping up like a jack-in-the-box, she leaned closer, all while remaining unobtrusive. Mel never once glanced at the camera, and Kara never called attention to herself or what she was doing.

He could watch her work all day. Whether she never acknowledged his presence or remained focused on the task before her, the concentration, skill, determination, and level of care she imparted on the job drew her even closer to his heart. Once she gave herself to something, nothing could shake her... unless it included speaking in front of a crowd.

*T*rent's constant attention left Kara equal parts frustrated and euphoric. He pressed a drink into her hand.

She gulped the punch and shoved the cup into his hand. Time for the real challenge.

Motioning for Darcy, Kara moved toward the flowering arbor Greener Gardens provided for the family photos. She pressed her shoulders down away from her ears and pasted on a smile. A quick look at Mel and the smile became genuine.

Darcy arrived with Mel's parents, and a flutter of panic blossomed in Kara's stomach. *You can do this.* Her gaze shifted once again to Mel, who offered an encouraging nod. *Right.*

"Mel, if you and Zeke would stand in the middle, I'd like to start with the bride's parents." Kara nodded at the Carmichaels and took a step back to frame the shot. Perfect.

She released the tension in her arms and called Zeke's parents forward. Forcing herself to only think about the next shot, Kara worked through the arrangements of parents, bridesmaids, groomsmen, and family in myriad combinations. Mel's brother hovered at the edge of the frame, forcing Kara to speak.

"Cooper, if you would take a step closer to Mel and let Darcy stand in front of you, I can get Miss Evelyn in this shot."

People shifted, doing as she asked and never complaining. When she finally released them, she scanned the crowd, only to find Trent watching her with a look of pride. Moving to the pavilion, Kara set up for the next segment. Dancing.

An hour later, the first dance complete and the happy couple off to change into their traveling clothes before setting off for the honeymoon, Kara found herself listless yet edgy. The freak combination drew her to the edge of the crowd after carefully returning her camera to its casing.

Trent's hand on her shoulder and his whispered plea for a dance cajoled her toward the dance floor.

Love songs.

Wedding bliss.

A man in wedding attire who smelled of pine and something lemony that reminded her of the animals he cared for with more determination than anyone she knew…Trent Raines completed a package she hadn't known to look for.

His arms wrapped around her waist, holding her closer than last time their feet slid along to a sappy beat.

The steady drum of his heart pulsed beneath his jaw, a tick-tock beat her own heart itched to match.

"You look beautiful." He whispered into her ear, his cheek pressed against hers.

Her hand convulsed and clenched a handful of shirt nestled between his shoulder blades. "You remember what I said last time we danced."

"I do. And I meant every word. Both times. There's no one else I'd rather dance with, and you are beautiful. Even if you don't know it." He gave her a twirl, his eyes lighting up when she gasped. "Maybe *because* you don't realize how gorgeous you are."

"Stop." Kara tucked her head against his shoulder.

His chuckle rumbled. "Spend enough time with me and you'll learn to accept compliments."

"If you manage to get snow for the festival, you can compliment me all you want."

"Somehow, I feel that's backward to how compliments are supposed to work."

"That's my final offer." Kara lifted her head and grinned. "Take it or leave it."

Another slow twirl, this one spinning her out and back into his embrace. His lips grazed her cheek. "I'll take it."

A low cheer spread through the awaiting guests as Darcy announced Mel and Zeke were heading toward the front door. Everyone scurried around the house, reminding Kara of a litter of puppies with a new toy. They lined the walkway, filling the space between Miss Evelyn's front door and Zeke's truck waiting on the curb.

Someone had already taken the pleasure of tying a string of tin cans to his trailer hitch and used chalk paint to scrawl "Just married" across the back glass.

With bags of flower petals in hand, Kara waited among the others for her first glimpse of the couple sans the bride and groom attire. Mel's simple dress matched Zeke's relaxed air of businessman gone casual with matching hues of blue.

Kara slid the camera from her bag, giving Trent a side glance before she slipped away and tucked herself at the end of the line. Trent slipped the bags from her hands, winking at the same time. He threw the petals high into the air. As they fluttered, drifting on the lazy ocean breeze, Kara clicked the shutter button.

Mel's laughter, the tilt of her chin when her head leaned back to bask in the showers of silken, falling roses, created an image Kara couldn't resist. A perfect ending to the joyful union of two hearts. And yet, this was not the end. Their beginning awaited. Their life as Mr. and Mrs. stretched out in an arching rainbow, and only God knew what waited on the other end of that bow.

Trent pressed a handkerchief into her free hand and took the camera. He cradled it to his chest, showing he understood how beloved the piece of equipment had become.

"People are supposed to cry at weddings, right?" She mopped her face, scowling at the streaks of mascara marring Trent's once white cloth. *Yeah right, waterproof mascara. Never buying into that crock again.*

"Depends on the reason, I suppose. If you're crying 'cause you're secretly madly in love with Zeke, then we might have a problem." Kara whacked his arm with the handkerchief, causing him to laugh before continuing. "But if you're crying because of the beautiful ceremony and the fact that two of your good friends are beginning the adventure of a lifetime…yeah, I think you can cry about that one."

His own voice sounded decidedly husky, and Kara squinted her eyes for a better look. "You're not crying because you're secretly in love with Mel, are you?"

"No." Trent coughed on the word and returned her camera, his shaking head not much reassurance to Kara's tender wedding feelings. "Friends only. Never anything more."

After repacking the Canon, Kara blew a strand of hair from her eyes and started to ask Trent to take her home when a loud squawk pierced the air. Kara ducked and threw both hands over her head.

Trent's hand landed on top of hers, the hard calluses and warm palm a contrast her body reacted to with an instinct nothing dared defy. A breath of cider-scented air carried Trent's reassurances. "It's only Bernie. Come to say goodbye, I suppose."

"The pelican? Gatecrashing a wedding? That's a new one." Kara lifted her head and searched the crowd for the source of another loud cry.

On the tail end of Bernie's vocal lament, a second voice

picked up, its human tone overwrought with parrot inflection as it flapped brilliant red and blue wings while wheeling overhead. "Lookout below!" Diving toward Darcy, the parrot mimicked the sound of a dive bomber before swooping back into the blue sky.

Bernie's indignant squawk and flapping wings meant he either disproved his friend's actions or merely wished for someone to toss him a fish.

Mel and Zeke waved from the truck windows, their faces glowing. "Need help?" Mel hung her head out the window.

Trent waved them on.

Darcy and Nigel corralled Bernie, who thought it rather impolite to be refrained from joining the newly wedded couple. The parrot soared back into view. "It's now or never, boys!" Tucking its wings, the bird shot like a missile, aiming for Darcy's face. Nigel pushed her behind him, forcing the bird to retreat once again.

"Now I've seen everything." Trent took Kara's hand, lacing their fingers together as he worked his way through the crowd. "It must have gotten lost during the hurricane."

"Sounds like it learned to talk from watching old war movies. I think I recognize some of the lines."

Most of the wedding guests disbanded the moment Zeke's truck rumbled out of sight. A few cast worried glances over their shoulders as the parrot continued wheeling and diving at intervals. Losing interest in Darcy, the parrot shot toward an unsuspecting guest and began peppering the air with sounds like bursts of gunfire.

Screaming, the woman flapped her arms, attempting to ward off the bird's sharp beak and talons, though the parrot never came close enough to cause any harm.

Trent surged ahead, pulling Kara along, while the screams of woman and bird reached ear-piercing levels.

Cooper jumped to the woman's defense, throwing himself in

front of the bird. The woman clutched the back of his shirt, her face buried in the space between his shoulder blades. Her shoulders rose and fell in heaving sobs.

Thank you, Lord, that this didn't happen any earlier.

Kara couldn't begin to imagine the catastrophe of having an unlikely pair of birds crashing the wedding party. Thank goodness Mel had the foresight to insist on an indoor ceremony.

"Where are we going?" Kara managed to keep stride with Trent, who raced toward his truck.

"Need a net." He increased his pace, breaking into a run when the woman screamed again.

Kara stumbled, her heels sinking into the soft earth. She released Trent's hand and waved him on when he turned back. "Go. I'll wait here. I can't run in heels."

He started to argue, the little line appearing between his eyebrows.

A surge of guests abandoning the house rocketed past. "Someone needs to catch that bird." One man growled while sending a frantic look over his shoulder.

Trent wavered.

Kara huffed and slid her shoes from her feet. Scooping them into her hand, she ran forward. "Let's go."

Relief removed the lines from Trent's face until he tried to push her into the truck after retrieving his net from behind the seat. "You'll be safe in here."

"I'm not getting in there." Slapping his hand away, she tucked her backpack into the floorboard and slammed the door. "Come on."

The line reappeared between his eyes.

"Would you rather stand here and argue with me while some poor stranger is getting attacked by a rogue bird?"

"Well..." Trent groaned and raked a hand through his hair. "When you put it like that. Fine. Let's go."

By the time they made it back to the squawking frenzy,

Bernie had taken to the air and was using his broad wingspan to keep the smaller parrot at bay.

omen. Trent bit off a grunt as he swung the net through the air, trying again, to catch the elusive parrot.

Kara stood off to the side, head tilted as she perused the scene with a thoughtful scrunch to her mouth.

He'd only wanted to protect her.

And she threw it in his face.

The rising anger caused a reckless swipe with the net, sending it close enough to Kara's face that she flinched back. Maybe next time, she'd listen. Unlikely.

He was being unfair. Regret and shame pulsed in heavy beats, along with a heavy dose of fear. The thought of seeing Kara hurt drove needle-sharp pains through him.

Swooping overhead, the parrot called out another inane line Trent recognized but couldn't place. Bernie cut the other bird off before it made another pass at Kara.

Cooper had hustled the woman he'd been protecting away once Trent arrived with the net. Returning, Cooper took up a vigilant position well out of Trent's range. *Must have seen that last attempt where you nearly decapitated your girl.*

No. Not his girl. He gave the net another mighty heave...and missed.

Someone gripped his shoulder. A touch he recognized with some inner peace that had been silent but roared to the surface with that gentle squeeze. "I don't think you're going to catch her like this." Kara wrapped her hand around the handle, her fingers grazing his. "She's frightened. And we're making it worse."

Going to do my job for me now too? The sarcastic comment stuck to his teeth. Kara didn't deserve his temper. He locked the words away, knowing he needed to examine them later to understand why the anger pushed so insistently against someone who'd done nothing but help since the moment she walked into his life.

Kara lifted her face to the sky, the curve of her chin jutting toward a flurry of feathers.

A desire to hold her in his arms flared to life. He followed her gaze. Spiraling against the backdrop of sky and clouds, the flapping wings beat an erratic tune.

Bernie circled, his squawks no longer loud and insistent but soothing. The parrot flitted toward the ground, only to be blocked by Bernie's impressive wings. Shooting upward, the two birds continued to whirl.

Trent lowered the net. "What do you think we should do?"

"Wait." Kara leaned against his arm, the softness of her dress brushing his knuckles. Her bare feet worked against the ground, an easy side-to-side motion that made her skirt twirl as it had when they danced.

Cooper approached, his heavy steps cutting through the soft swish of grass against Kara's feet. With a cry, the parrot dove.

Trent started to raise the net. Kara's hand gripped his, tight enough to pinch the knuckles together. "Wait."

"She's going to attack him."

"No. She won't." Kara squeezed his forearm. "Trust me."

Why? What did she see in the parrot that he missed? Trent looked up again.

Throwing out its wings, the bird slowed its descent and landed on Cooper's shoulder. Nuzzling his cheek with its head, the parrot uttered what sounded like a human sigh.

"Cooper? What's the deal, man?" Trent stabbed the net handle into the ground and glared.

Bernie gave a cry and landed at Cooper's feet. Giving what could only be a derisive shake of his wings, the pelican sat and eyed his feathery friend.

"No idea." Cooper tried to shake his head, but the parrot had taken hold of his ear with her beak. "I've seen her around with Bernie when I'm out on the boat, but she's never come close before." He reached up, holding out a finger, and the parrot hopped onto it. "You know who owns her?"

"Not a clue." Trent gripped the net, a lifeline to anchor a swirling coil of tension. "You can bring her to the shelter. I'll have Kendall check her out and ask around for an owner."

Cooper flashed a grin when the little bird walked up his arm and settled in by his ear. "Sure. I'll take her home with me. There's an old cage in the garage I can use." He flicked a glance between Trent and Kara. "You should hit the waves today. Great day for paddling out to deep water."

"Yeah. Maybe." Trent shrugged off the sudden change in topic.

"Where's the woman you were shielding?" Kara shot the question at Cooper.

Shrugging carefully to keep from dislodging the parrot, Cooper answered, "No idea. Don't even know who she is."

The parrot squawked and flapped. "Looking good, boys."

"Why don't you take her home before she flies off again." Trent backed away, holding out his hand for Kara. If she refused it, he wouldn't be surprised. His attitude the last hour stank worse than an uncleaned kennel.

Once out of Cooper's hearing, Kara tugged on his arm. "Why are you upset with me?"

Well. So much for the idea her shy nature held her back from conflict. Seemed that only worked with a crowd.

"I'm not."

Her harrumph rivaled the little old women at church when they'd been told the potluck was cancelled because of the incoming hurricane.

"Really. I...why wouldn't you stay in the truck where it was safe?"

"That's what you're upset about? Because I wouldn't hide and let you take care of the problem alone?" Kara blew out a short breath before she chuckled. "Well, that's a relief. I thought you were regretting ever asking to drive me over today."

Her thought process rambled around so many tracks his head spun. "Never crossed my mind. I didn't want you to get hurt."

"I might fall to pieces if you asked me to give a wedding speech, but facing down a parrot...I deserve a little more credit. I've handled dogs a hundred times bigger and meaner than that bird." She poked a finger at his shoulder. "And the snake. Don't forget the snake. You wouldn't come out of your office until I got rid of it. My first day on the job and I wrangled a snake because you couldn't."

"Now you're being petty, bringing up all my faults."

"I think it's adorable. Macho dog guru can't stand the sight of a snake. Not even a photo."

She had him there. He'd rather eat scorpions than look at a snake. "You want to go kayaking with me?"

The question surprised her, if the slack jaw meant anything, but she recovered quick enough to bob her head before one of the long, often awkward pauses he'd come to expect from her.

"Okay then. Let's go." Ushering her back to the truck, she slid onto the seat this time without any argument.

"Would it be safe to take the camera?"

"No promises. I've dumped myself out of the kayak more times than I can count. You know how to swim, right?" Trent shut the door on her sputtering indignation that of course she could swim.

A short drive to his house, then a hop over to hers, and they were on their way to the beach with a pair of kayaks strapped in the back of the truck and a pair of huskies shoving their heads through the narrow window between him and Kara.

Kara stuck her arm out the window, moving it up and down in slow waves that set Remus to bounding forward and ramming his nose into her face. Pushing him back, she wiped a line of slobber from her cheek. "What about them? Can't leave them alone on the beach while we paddle out."

"They'll ride with me." Trent clicked the blinker and made a turn onto a winding, sandy road where the crash of ocean surf began a steady cadence. "The only time those two are ever still is when they're in the kayak. They love it." He ruffled Remus' ears before pushing the dog's head away.

Putting the truck in park, Trent faced Kara. "I'm sorry for how I acted earlier. You didn't deserve that."

"Forgiven and forgotten." Kara patted his shoulder, her expression open enough for him to see she meant the words.

From kissing, to a wedding, to a crazy parrot...what next?

Letting the dogs out, Trent started working on the kayaks while Kara chased after the rowdy pups. Romulus bounced upward, his vertical jump impressive for his age. Reaching Kara's shoulder, the red and white furball snapped his teeth at the spray of sand Kara's heels churned up.

When she picked up a piece of driftwood and waved it, both dogs lowered their front ends, then sprung straight up. Kara gave the stick a hurl, and the dogs shot after the flying debris with a joyful yip.

You have to find them a new home. They're ready.

They were, but he wasn't. More than any other foster, Remus and Romulus worked their way into his heart. Getting them out would be no small feat.

And Kara. Trent cast a look her way and caught her staring back. No more kissing Kara. Not without a date first.

128

22

Wiping sweat from her cheek, Kara made the last swipe of off-white paint over the red slashes splashed across Trent's house.

She dropped the paintbrush onto the tray and tried to tame her hair as Trent's truck rolled down the drive, but only succeeded in spreading paint across her forehead and into the wisps dancing about her face. Groaning at the injustice of meeting him this way, Kara plastered a smile on her face that felt as unnatural as shooting in the dark.

Trent heralded his approach with jingling keys. The clink stopped, sending silence over the yard. Remus and Romulus, asleep after a full hour of fetch, didn't bother to lift their heads from dual sentry positions beside the front door.

"You should see your face right now!" Nigel jogged toward Trent and slapped a paint-covered hand over his shoulder, leaving a smear of white on Trent's forest green polo.

"You painted my house." His tone suggested amazement.

Kara checked his expression, the tight lines around his mouth, and moved on to his hands shoved deep into pockets and feet that seemed anchored to the ground. Maybe this had been a bad idea. Or a good idea done at the wrong time. Trent seemed in no frame of mind to accept a favor, no matter how small.

Nigel—oblivious to Trent's discomfort—waved a hand in Kara's direction. "It was Kara's idea. She organized the whole thing."

Thanks, Nigel. Way to throw me under the bus.

She couldn't be angry at him, though. All the responsibility deserved to fall on her shoulders.

Darcy trotted to Nigel and mouthed "Sorry" when she flew by.

What could Kara do but offer a reassuring nod that all was well? Stooping to pick up her tools and empty paint can, Kara shuffled everything together. The remaining people—Beth, Sam, and others Kara lost track of dropped their paint brushes in with hers.

She managed to thank them all and say goodbye without her voice quivering or sounding like she'd finished a three-mile hike on a trail that ran straight uphill. Small progress, but progress, nonetheless.

Then, between securing a paint lid and reaching for another, Trent's feet appeared at the same time the lid she needed flew from her hand. Kara lunged after it and slammed her head into Trent's knees. He rocked back with a grunt.

Rubbing her head, Kara snatched the lid and tried to shimmy backward. Remus woke with a yip and bounded onto her back. The impact sent her sprawling face-first into the dirt. Her breath left in a whoosh, and she sucked in a lungful of dirt before turning her head and spitting out grit.

"Remus! Down." Trent's harsh order caused the pup to whine, but the weight dropped from her back. "Are you okay?"

His arm looped under her armpit and she had a brief flash of agony over whether he could feel the sweat sliding down her skin.

"Fine." Her voice resembled Kermit the Frog with a hint of exasperation. She tried to pull her arm away, but Trent hauled her upright and held her there. "I'm okay."

"Your nose is bleeding."

So that's why she sounded like a Muppet. She tilted her head back and gagged as a trickle of coppery blood ran down her throat.

"Here, sit down." Trent guided her to the side and pressed a hand to her shoulder.

Her backside hit the steps with a resounding thud at the same time the screen door screeched open, and Trent's dad emerged with a tray of glasses. "Trent, you're home! Kara, what on earth happened to you?"

"Don't eat the dirt." She tried to quip, but it came out morose and watery all at the same time.

Trent shot into the house, returning with a towel in one hand and an ice pack in the other. He pressed the towel into her hand and sat down, bouncing the boards with the weight of his body. "Lean your head forward. Hold that to your nose. I'm going to rest this against your eyes and the bridge of your nose. Maybe you won't bruise."

Mr. Raines settled on Kara's other side after lowering the tray to the boards. He patted her knee, the touch as reassuring as her own father's. "Even if you do bruise, it'll go away soon enough."

"How did this happen?" Trent winced when he looked at her. Not a good sign.

"You were there, you saw how it happened."

"Not this"—he waved toward her face then at the house— "this. The house. I thought you were sick today."

Talking hurt, but not as much as the doubt clouding his eyes and the sudden pressure of his hand against her face. He'd allowed the ice pack to slip below her eyes, giving her a full view of his twisted expression.

"I never said I was sick."

His mouth flew open as though to refute her.

"I said I needed the day off and since all the animals had already been photographed and uploaded to the website, I had some other things to take care of."

"I assumed you meant...You know..." His face flushed a brilliant shade of red, and even his dad couldn't mistake the meaning behind the blushing cheeks. Trent cleared his throat and tried again. "How long have you been planning this and how did you know I wouldn't come home early?"

Kara nearly snorted before realizing how much it would hurt, not to mention probably restart the blood trickling from her nose. "You never leave work early. In the year we've worked together, not once have you left the building a second before closing time. You even worked last winter with the flu and sent me home instead." She poked a finger at him, doing nothing more than hurting her own knuckle when she landed on the solidness of his shoulder.

Pressure built across the bridge of her nose, and each breath whistled.

Mr. Raines cleared his throat, a gentle reprimand or the irritation of the nip in the air, Kara had no way of knowing.

Trent, however, cast a glance at his dad and nodded once. "Thank you for doing this. It was a nice gesture. I'm sorry for sounding ungrateful. You surprised me. That's all."

"Doh probleb." Hearing her mangled words, she leaned back to probe her swollen nose. "Oh doy." Tender flesh met her fingertips, and Trent's shocked look sent Kara rocketing to her feet before she discovered the extent of her problem. "I dotta doh."

"Kara, wait." He reached out, drawing her to a halt while he stood. "Can you even see to drive home?"

"Yes." Good. At least one word came out plain. Surely by the time she reached the road the swelling would clear.

"Uh-huh." Trent's lips twitched.

"It's dot fuddy." She groaned and pressed her lips together.

"Why don't you drive Kara home? I'll follow in my car and bring you back."

Kara tried to wave off Mr. Raines suggestion, but—like his son—a hardness had settled over his voice that said he'd not be dissuaded from his path.

"It's the least I can do to repay you for painting my house." Trent held out his hand, wiggling the first two fingers. "Hand over those keys…unless you'd like to stay for dinner?"

"Great idea." Mr. Raines backpedaled, a smile pulling deep grooves into his cheeks. "I'll cook."

This man hadn't found much to smile about in recent years. Tight lines bracketing his eyes eased when he chuckled.

The two men looked at one another as though agreeing with each other was a foreign concept.

Father and son, different and yet so alike as they chuckled and squared off against Kara.

Dinner with Trent…and his dad. Fun, or a disaster waiting to happen?

Kara rolled the idea around. Since humiliation seemed to follow her anyway, what harm could she possibly find in sitting down to a simple meal?

"Sure." One shoulder lifted in what she hoped looked like a casual shrug. The swelling between her eyes left things a little blurry around the edges and a tight pressure lodged between her brows.

Testing to see whether he was still in trouble, Remus crept forward and whined. Romulus bounced, all four paws leaving the ground as he shot up like an arrow reaching for the sky.

Trent blocked the pups from reaching Kara, his side pressing against her stomach and chest as he ordered the dogs to sit. They obeyed, but tails swishing and yowling accompanied the order.

Kara sniggered once before the pain in her face halted the sound. "Ow."

Trent handed her the ice pack, his touch gentle. "Come on in."

"I should go." Mr. Raines juggled a set of keys in his hand, something close to mischief dancing in his eyes and the smile she thought of as Trent's hand-in-the-cookie-jar smile showing off swoon-worthy dimples.

"Oh no." Trent's head jerked toward his father. "You promised to cook. And you have to follow me when I drive Kara home after dinner."

Allowing Trent to lead her into the house, it wasn't until they were sitting on the couch that Kara remembered the tight quarters. Trent pressed against her side, every joint giving off a spark of heat.

Mr. Raines bumped around in the kitchen, a happy whistle soaring while a hint of rosemary tickled the air.

"Sorry about your nose."

"It's oday." Kara shook her head. Yeah. Dinner with Trent wouldn't be a disaster at all considering she couldn't even talk without sounding ridiculous.

23

*a*fter a delightful meal, Trent delivered Kara safely home and saw her to the door before allowing the ride back with his dad to send thoughts scurrying.

His dad drove the same way he did everything in life, with slow precision and a do-it-right-the-first-time attitude. He kept his attention focused on the road ahead, but something lingered between them, as real and tangible as the leather seat and nylon seatbelt pressing hard against Trent's chest.

Constricted…and conflicted…he roughed his hand over the smooth seat cover and began. "Dad—"

"I like that Kara." The interruption—perfectly timed—said more than the four words uttered. "I see why you're in such a pickle. Girl like that doesn't come around very often."

"Unless you live around here." Trent motioned toward the beach hovering out of sight. "Noticed all the couples lately? Marriages popping up all over the place like one of those boutique shops women are all agog over."

"True." A head nod punctuated the point. "But it's not like any of those women were right for you."

"You're talking about soulmates."

135

"You don't believe in them?"

Did he? He'd never thought about it much. His parents were a perfect example. But he knew countless others who'd not been so lucky. Kara's face danced through his mind, calling the answer from his heart. "I think I do. But how do you know you've found the right one?"

"If you have to ask, then you haven't. That's how it was for me, anyway. And your mother. I couldn't imagine living the rest of my life without her."

They rode in silence after that. Trent's mind whirled with new information, processing, discarding, and organizing what he knew into the empty spaces of what might be. His desire to apologize, again, for his actions fell into a forgotten box and allowed him to simply enjoy the drive.

After they pulled into Trent's drive and he waved goodbye to his dad, Trent retreated to the backyard where the two husky pups raced each other around the fence perimeter. He needed exercise, something to take his mind off the idea of love and soulmates and forever.

He ran the dogs independently, taking each one around the obstacle course once per turn. Remus hesitated at the tunnel, no doubt restless about the darkness settling around them. Trent crouched at the opposite end, his voice calm as he called Remus forward. With a whine, the pup jumped, his paws scrabbling on the slick material until he shot into Trent's arms.

"Good boy." He patted, praised, and offered a treat to the excited pup before asking him to move on to his favorite obstacle, the rope bridge. Here, the dog had to traverse two ropes, spread wide enough and taut enough that the dog's paws could reach across and have enough tension to sway but not stretch so far the animal fell.

Remus lowered a paw to the rope and steadied himself before placing the other. He focused on the path before him, ignoring all other sights either behind or beside him. Trust, in himself and in Trent, gave the pup courage. Learning to creep over the bridge while searching for danger would come later.

"They're moving right along." Nigel swung the gate open and patted Romulus on the side.

"Look what the tide dragged in." Trent gave a hand signal for Remus to wait and the dog dropped to his belly. One of his most hated orders.

Nigel ran his fingers through his beard, a sure sign of uncertainty. "Darcy sent me."

"Okay." Trent drew out the word when Nigel didn't explain.

Starting to pace, Nigel slapped his palms together. "I saw the pictures Kara took. Great shots, by the way, but not why I'm here."

Nigel paced, and Trent waited. Guessing games were so not his wheelhouse. Dogs needing training, sure. Men and their love lives, which he was assuming was the real reason behind Nigel showing up, leagues outside his skill level.

"Am I making a mistake?"

Trent folded his arms and kept waiting.

"Marriage? Marrying Darcy? Is it a mistake?"

"Man, you've been waiting for nearly two decades to marry that girl, and now that you have a ring on her finger, you're getting cold feet? Unbelievable."

"It's not that." Nigel snapped, the words sharp in the darkness highlighted here and there with the work lamps Trent clamped onto the fence when they did these nighttime runs. Nigel's shadow bobbed like a drunken sailor. "I don't deserve her."

"Too late for that." He cringed at the thoughtless comment and threw up a hand. "Ignore that. Not what I meant."

Nigel froze, only his eyes moving as he searched Trent's face.

"Darcy loves you with a love powerful enough to write novels about. Deserving love has nothing to do with it. We didn't deserve God's love. We still don't. If we all got what we deserved, the world would be a terrible place. Even worse than it is now. You two love each other. Trust that love. Trust God with what He's given you and love Darcy with every breath. Even when it's hard. Because there will be times when it won't be easy."

"I know."

"You needed someone to say it." Trent reached out to shake Nigel's hand. "Long as you invite me to the wedding. Maybe name a kid after me, and we'll be even."

"Now that you mention it. The best man's spot is still open. I've been saving it for someone." Nigel tapped a fingertip to his temple. "Now, who did I want to be my best man? Oh, that's right. It was you." He slapped a hand on Trent's shoulder. "Can't wait to see you in a monkey suit."

"Thanks, but no thanks." The joke fell on deaf ears.

"You're welcome." Nigel chortled. "I know how much you were looking forward to impressing Kara."

"You'd know a lot about that, what with all the lengths you went through for Darcy." Trent whistled for Remus, and the husky bounded to his feet. "Let's go, pirate, see if those sea legs are good for anything other than dancing."

Nigel took up the challenge with a haughty lift of his chin. "I'll have you know, Shep is a master of the obstacle course."

"Your sheepdog couldn't walk a plank if it was as wide as my truck."

"And your huskies couldn't herd sheep if I tied ropes around their necks and led them to the corral."

Trent snorted. "There aren't even any sheep on the Islands."

"Got me there." Nigel slapped his leg, drawing Romulus to his side. "Let's see how the two of them work together."

Letting his friend take the lead, Trent relaxed against the metal fence and appreciated the graceful lines of the dogs in motion. From his normal standpoint, he missed this view, usually only seeing the dogs from beside him.

From here, their strengths emerged. Romulus faltered on the see-saw, jumping off at the midway point when the wooden board began to teeter. Remus ran to the middle and yipped, as though saying the trick was easy and his brother had given up too soon.

Romulus whined but remained on the ground, waiting.

"Good boy, Remus." Nigel encouraged when the pup scrambled to the ground and raced toward the tunnel.

Not long ago, Nigel's experience with the course was nonexistent. But, like his turnaround with Darcy, he'd decided to learn something new, pushing the boundaries of knowledge and accepting that the future held more than a past mistake.

Trent made a note of the similarities in their history. Different mistakes and outcomes, but both leading them to a place where they struggled to accept themselves as worthy.

Unlike Trent's choice to leave the Island and become a criminal, Nigel's mistake had been the result of something outside his control. An accident.

Actions. Reactions. Consequences.

The possibilities swirled into a muddy mess every time he tried to look deeper.

"You look constipated." Nigel bumped his fist against Trent's stomach. "Need a little boost?"

"You're disgusting."

"Now you sound like Darcy."

"You calling me a girl?" Trent pushed Nigel's shoulder, rocking the man back on his heels.

"Just calling it like I see it." Nigel pushed back, then swept his leg out, knocking Trent's feet from the ground.

He landed with a thud, Remus and Romulus there in a heartbeat to offer slobbery kisses. "Off, you mutts."

"Hey now, you'll offend their sensitivities. You can't go calling purebred huskies mutts."

"Now who sounds like a girl?" Trent smirked and held his hand out for Nigel to pull. "Gimme a hand, you great big bloke."

"Nothing like name calling to honor your best friend. I can always take back that offer to be best man."

"Feel free." Trent mimed a noose around his neck. "If you're gonna make me wear a tie, I ain't going."

24

*T*wo weeks. Kara eyed the Christmas tree and chewed on the cap of her ink pen. Two weeks to pull together the Christmas Festival. Her checklist beckoned from beneath the canvas backpack. She knew what it said. On track. Not late. Not ahead of schedule.

One foul-up had the potential to put the entire operation at risk. And she was spending her Saturday night at the animal shelter playing decorator instead of at home planning.

Blowing a strand of hair from her eyes, Kara tossed the pen on top of the stack of lists and pulled an ornament from the box. She stretched onto her tiptoes, trying to hook the red ornament to one of the uppermost branches on Forever Pals' Christmas tree.

"I think it might actually make you break out in hives to ask for help." Trent swiped the ornament from her hand and settled it on the exact branch she wanted.

"Hard to ask someone who spends his mornings locked away in his office." Kara popped a hand to her hip and tried out a flirty smile. *Really, Kara? Flirting.*

Trent's eyes took on a dazed look.

Not knowing whether the expression meant the flirting worked, or if he suddenly developed a bout of wondering if she'd lost her mind, Kara dropped her hand and reached for another ornament.

Unfortunately, all the lower branches were covered with plastic depictions of every imaginable animal and some that left room for the imagination to roam. Kara reached again, aiming this time for a branch on the row below the one Trent used.

"If you fall into that tree because you're too stubborn to say 'Here, put this on the tree for me' then I'm going to let you clean up the mess *and* redecorate the whole thing all by yourself." The low chuckle nixed the stern tone Trent adopted. Hands on his hips, he shook his head at her outstretched pose.

"Here. Put this on the tree for me." Kara shoved the ornament at his chest, her knuckles bumping him in the process. Complete accident. *Keep telling yourself that.*

"Now, was that so hard?"

"You have no idea." Kara passed him another from the box and pointed at the branch where she thought it would look best.

Trent hooked the golden orb on a branch far to the left of where she indicated.

With a smack to his hand, Kara removed the ornament, used his arm for balance, and placed it in the bare spot above her head. "You're messing up the vision." She motioned at the small tree occupying the corner of the room across from the check-in desk. The green needles and bright baubles popped against the dull gray walls.

"You're messing up my head." Trent's lips buzzed her temple. "You smell like cocoa. How do you smell like cocoa?"

"Anybody home?" Cooper strode into the lobby, pulling the door closed behind him and lugging a large cage. "Clean bill of health for the parrot. Sorry I didn't make it earlier. Work's insane, but Kendall checked out the bird for me right after I took it home."

142

From what Kara gleaned from Mel, Cooper operated a small boat business. He spent his days on the water, ferrying passengers from island to island when they couldn't—or didn't want to —drive. If things were slow on the residential islands, he tootled up to Mimosa and took on boat tours for vacationers.

"Bombs away!" The parrot squawked and flapped its wings. Cooper flicked the covering back over the parrot's cage, effectively silencing the bird. For now.

"No problem." Trent's hand slapped against Cooper's shoulder and the bird squawked again.

"Kara, I'll help you with the tree in a bit." He blinked at her and clasped his hands beneath his chin. "Will you help me?"

The comical effect, or maybe it was flirting, skated through her.

He made it sound so easy. As though asking for help was something he did every day and held no more power over a person than saying "Great coffee" when the waitress came by to refill a cup. Why couldn't she do that?

The ornament dropped from her hand and landed in the box with a *plink*. "Not sure how much help I'll be, but sure."

Cooper followed Trent down the short hallway and into his office, while Kara nudged the box of ornaments into a safer position beneath a chair. Silence closed in, the animals quiet as they settled into the night. Thick concrete walls helped muffle the sounds of a hundred animals in identical kennels one hallway away.

The bells she'd hung on the door this morning jingled, signaling someone's entrance. All the employees had already been sent home, leaving Trent and Kara to manage what little business trickled in at the late hour.

Trent's head popped out from the office, and Kara waved him back. "I'll take care of it. You go ahead."

Trent waved his thanks and retreated.

"Well now, this is a surprise."

Kara froze, her feet becoming one with the concrete as the oily voice slid over her skin. A samba beat took up residence in her ears. Turning took effort. More than it should, and as the profile of the man came into view, she let out a squeak.

"You remember me." The burly man from the volunteer shelter took a step forward.

Snake. This had to be him. Though Trent never showed her the picture from the license the dogs found, no one else met the criteria for smarmy, snake-like, dog-fighting gang member vibe that this man possessed. And Trent told Christian after the ferry ride that Snake was at Marco's place.

"Let's have a tour. Shall we?" He reached for her arm. "I'd like to adopt some animals."

"I don't think you're what we're looking for." Kara took a step back, out of reach.

The man snarled, causing the snake tattoo along the side of his neck to coil and writhe. Yep. No doubt in her mind. This man had bad news scrawled over every inch, and not because most of the skin showing was covered in ink. He oozed spite and venom with every breath.

"Wasn't a question." He advanced, meaty hands clamping around her arm.

Kara shrieked, the sound coming from her mouth surprising even her with its intensity.

The man flinched, his hand lifting. No doubt to either strike her or clap over her mouth to stop the unyielding sound.

Kara swung her arm, knocking her fist into his shoulder and pushing her body into motion. The man didn't budge save for the narrowing of his eyes. She spun on her heel, elbow popping with the force of his hold.

Trent bolted from the office, his momentum slamming him against the opposite wall before he recovered and raced toward her with Cooper on his heels.

A hiss of breath from behind, followed by the bells' jingle

and a brush of salty air slowed Kara's headlong flight into Trent. He cradled her against his chest, his heart thundering in her ear.

Cooper raced on, following the man into the parking lot. Tires spun, the squeal of rubber sharp and insistent.

"Did he hurt you?" Trent's chest vibrated, his voice rumbling deep with worry.

Cooper returned, phone pressed against his ear as he repeated a series of letters and numbers.

"Kara." Trent ran his hands over her back, drawing out a shiver. "Did he hurt you?"

She shook her head, not yet trusting her voice as she found security in Trent's arms. Heat bloomed in her chest, a desire to know she could always run to him and be accepted.

"Christian's on his way." Cooper slapped a hand on the wall.

The sound jolted through Kara like an electric current. Trent hugged her tighter, letting her melt into the heat and strength emanating from the embrace. His tenderness pressed against the holes, soothing the bits of emptiness and filling them with hope.

Is this the love You have for Your children? Her throat burned with the question. How long since she had felt so loved and accepted? *Did I push You away, God?* What would it be like to rest in the comfort of her heavenly Father with absolute trust? She loved God. Served Him. Had He truly stopped listening...or had she simply stopped trusting that God loved her as much as He loved all His children? *God, I want to run to You with absolute trust, knowing You will hold and protect me.*

Trent murmured in her ear, drawing Kara away from her inquiry.

She backed away, wiping her eyes and sniffling back the tears. "I'll be in your office." Waving away Trent's concern, Kara retreated to the solid room where his presence lingered on every dusty surface and cluttered stack. Her fingers twitched, ready to dive into the mess and put it to rights. To do something to tame the chaos tumbling through her veins. If only feelings could be sorted, categorized, organized, and put into boxes where they could be removed when needed and returned when no longer of use.

Moving a stack of adoption applications, Kara uncovered Trent's Bible. First John chapter four and verse eighteen glared at her from beneath purple highlighter. "There is no fear in love; but perfect love casteth out fear: because fear hath torment. He that feareth is not made perfect in love."

Perfect love.

Her fingertips trailed over the words. Her eyes closed, a prayer on her lips.

The door snapped open. Christian, Trent, and Cooper strode in, filling the room with testosterone and fury.

Kara sagged into a chair.

"All right. Kara, tell me what happened."

With Trent's hand on her shoulder, Kara bolstered her flagging strength as the adrenaline fled her system and started at the moment she heard the bells on the door. Christian listened, waiting until she finished to ask questions.

At the end, he tapped his thigh and scowled. "We'll track him down. Cooper got the plate number. You should go home and rest."

Kara's head bobbled her agreement, though her stomach rumbled a complaint. Food first. Then sleep.

25

*T*rent squeezed Kara's shoulder, feeling the knots of tension beneath his fingers. She didn't deserve to get caught up in his mess. "Come on, I'll take you home."

A look bounced between Cooper and Christian as Kara stood and wrapped her arms around her stomach.

"Where's your truck?" Cooper motioned toward the small window facing the parking lot. "I didn't see any vehicles when I pulled in. Thought for a minute no one was here."

Right. He'd walked to work this morning, needing the exercise to work off the anticipation of an extra day with Kara.

"Why don't both of you get off the Island for a bit?" Christian pushed himself out of the chair and hitched his utility belt up. "I'm not saying it isn't safe for you to go home. Snake probably found a hole to crawl into and won't come out for a while, but you look like you could use some fun. Have Cooper drive you home, then you and Kara run up to Mimosa for some dinner. Forget about all this for a bit and relax."

No. The word rested on Trent's tongue. He needed to keep Kara at a distance, away from the danger and repercussions of his past. *Your actions. Your responsibility.*

147

"I've never eaten there." Kara shifted her feet, bringing her arm close enough to brush his.

"Where?" Cooper's confused expression was no doubt mirrored on Trent's face.

Kara glanced around the room, her eyes growing wide. "Mimosa."

"Not *anywhere* on Mimosa?" Incredulous, Christian crossed his arms, his voice rising. "That's it. Trent, I'm ordering you to take this girl to dinner. We can't let this stand. Poor girl's been on Hopper for a year and hasn't sampled the tourist trap island." He cast a focused look at Kara. "You've been to Beth's food truck, though, right? Please tell me you haven't been missing out on the best parts of our Islands."

"Oh, yeah. I stop by Beth's anytime I can. Never saw the need to go all the way up to Mimosa."

"Something we must remedy immediately. It's criminal to miss out on Mimosa." Christian opened the office door and waved a hand. "Go. Now. Mimosa's calling."

Trent took Kara's hand, reveling in the feel of her fingers entwined with his. Who knew holding hands could elicit such deep feelings of rightness and belonging?

Kara remained quiet through the journey from the animal shelter to Trent's home, the two of them squished together with Cooper in his single cab truck. No room—or reason—to complain since Trent rather enjoyed the closeness that pressed her into his side and gave him an excuse to drape his arm over her shoulder.

Cooper idled in the drive behind Trent's truck, headlights on and bathing the freshly painted bungalow in warm light. "There's a great little place off the docks on Mimosa. 'Bout a block from the pirate tour boats. If you ask me, that's where you should go. Not as loud as some places but heavy with the flavor of the Islands."

"I know the place." Trent helped Kara from the truck and bumped fists with Cooper. "Thanks for the ride."

"Enjoy your date."

Trent didn't bother correcting Cooper, who was too busy backing out onto the road to pay much attention. This didn't count as a date...did it? Not when they were forced into it under pain of Christian's demands. Then again, if Trent counted it as a date, he could justify a goodnight kiss when he dropped Kara off.

Across the Islands, over the bridges where the moonlight glittered on the ocean like diamonds seeking the flicker of lantern light in a black cave, they traveled with only the gentle thrum of music to break the silence. On Breaker's, they waited for a boat to finish the journey.

"You would have told me if you didn't want to go to dinner, wouldn't you?" He should have asked earlier, but his own yearning to spend time with Kara drowned out the niggle of doubt until they were closer to Mimosa.

"Of course." Kara crossed her legs and shifted around to face him.

He kept his attention on the water but allowed his peripheral vision to track her movements. Relief, pure and sweet, filled his heart. She wanted to spend time with him. Even knowing who he'd been, the yuck that made up his past, Kara stayed by his side.

After her flight into his arms earlier, he'd dared to dream, but only as far as the weight of responsibility allowed. Shackles he'd allowed to hold him back eased open, teasing with a chance to escape their clutches and leave the prison of holding on to the past.

They rolled into the restaurant's parking lot—courtesy of a rented golf cart—the bloom of neon and fluorescent casting harsh bars of light across the asphalt.

"Should I wait for you to open my door? You seem rather

partial to it since coming back from that first trip." Kara grinned, breaking the tension, as she motioned at the emptiness.

His breath whooshed out with a chuckle, and he leaped into character. "Yep. Sit tight." He raced around to her side and held out a hand. "You may alight, my dear."

"Someone's been practicing."

Trent turned in time to catch Mel elbowing Zeke. "Did he get those lines from you? Sounds like something Rhett Butler would say."

"Don't fall for it, Trent." Zeke warded off Mel's playful jabs. "They'll tell you they hate those sappy lines, but secretly, way down deep inside, it makes them melt into little puddles of goo."

"Did he say Mel melts into puddles of poo?" Kara whisper-shouted loud enough for the newlywed couple to hear.

"Kara! I didn't know you had it in you." Mel swooped in and looped her arm through Kara's. "Excellently placed pun."

"I find it curious that we left your brother, and we *happen* to run into you two at the restaurant he recommended." Trent took Kara's other arm.

Mel's smile gleamed. "Probably because we're the ones who told him we were coming here tonight since Mom and Dad are gone for the weekend and we're not having our regular Saturday family dinner."

"Would you like to join us?" Zeke wiggled an eyebrow at Trent and opened the door for Mel. "We'd appreciate the company."

"Yeah, because having dinner with newlyweds won't be an exercise in avoiding sappy looks and gag-worthy romantic overtures." Trent attempted to sound disgusted, but the laughter from the couple in question ruined his effect.

"Speak for yourself. Romance is only dead if you allow it to be." Kara tossed her ponytail and squeezed Trent's arm. "I think you're a closet romantic. The louder you protest, the deeper your feelings on the subject. I bet you bought your girlfriends flowers for every date."

Roasted. Skewer him with a bamboo stick and place him over the fire. He'd been discovered.

Zeke didn't bother covering his boisterous laughter. He slapped a hand against Trent's shoulder. "Welcome to the dark side."

"We have coffee!" Mel lobbed the final insult over her shoulder.

"I hope it's a Darth roast." Kara quipped.

Her response left Trent with aching sides as laughter tightened his muscles until he couldn't breathe.

Their hostess, a twenty-something woman with blue hair and a nose ring tipped up glittering lips and waved a handful of plastic menus. "I can tell you'll fit right in around here." She led them past captain's wheels mounted to the walls and row upon row of pirate paraphernalia from treasure chests to peg legs and around to a circular booth tucked into the back of the restaurant.

Kara scooted into the booth, making little bounces with each move. Her cheeks blushed a deep rose when Trent slid in beside her and dangled a gold-tassled napkin over her lap.

The hostess retreated with a promise their waiter would be by soon.

Mel dissolved into giggles, with Kara following suit soon after.

Trent caught Zeke's attention and rolled his eyes, but they both smiled until Trent's cheeks ached. He'd needed this release. A few moments of fun to balance the scales.

"Have you heard the one about the pirate?" Zeke leaned forward, his elbows on the table and chin propped on his knuckles.

Mel groaned. "No. You're not spending the entire night telling bad jokes."

"My jokes are not bad…They're punny." He said it with such a deadpan expression that Trent had to take the words through his mind again.

Kara pressed her shoulder into Trent's, her expression vulnerable yet courageous. "What do you call a hairy pirate?"

"A Wookie!" Zeke jabbed his finger at Mel. "You get it, right? *Star Wars?* Chewbacca is a Wookie and he and Han Solo are space pirates."

"Yes. Yes. You don't have to explain." Mel waved Zeke away, her words rolling out between spasms of laughter.

Trent wrapped his arm around Kara's waist, pulling her against his side. She leaned in and rested her head against his shoulder. And he knew. He'd fallen in love with her. No one else drew out the joy of a moment and touched his heart the way she did.

By the time he dropped her off at her house, dreams of the future slammed hard and fast, begging to be set loose. He pressed a gentle kiss to her cheek, not trusting himself enough to offer more. Not yet. Soon. From his prayers to God's ears.

*K*ara approached Forever Pals with anticipation, sweaty palms, and a smile. An eerie silence cloaked the building. She shuddered while reaching for the door, only to be thrown off balance when Trent blocked her way.

A heavy voice called out from the main aisle. "Might as well let her in, Trent."

Trent's eyes hardened, the blue glint turning cold. "She had nothing to do with this." He swiveled back to face her. "No work today, Kara. Go home."

"No way." She tried to step forward, but Trent refused to move. "What's going on? Why is it so quiet?"

"There's been a break-in."

Kara put her palm on Trent's chest and pushed. "Are the dogs okay? Did they take anything?" Her momentum, and possibly the surprise of her insistence, forced Trent back a step. She squeezed between him and the door frame, coming face to face with Deputy Johnson. "Did anyone get hurt?"

Trent took her hand, slowing her steps and offering support to her race toward the too quiet hallway. Empty. Every cage.

"They're all gone? Where? How?" Kara spun a slow circle, attempting to organize the whirling thoughts. "Trent. What happened? Are Remus and Romulus okay?"

"They're fine. Safe at my house." Trent rubbed his hand over her back, offering comfort.

Johnson tapped his cell phone against his palm, then hitched his sagging jeans up over his hip. "When was the last time you were here?"

"Saturday. But you know that. You were here then too." Kara pulled her gaze back, locking it onto the badge clipped on Johnson's belt. She volleyed back to Trent. "I don't understand. Who would do this?"

"Snake." Trent's lip curled in a way that transformed his entire face into a mask of anger and resentment.

"Now, we don't know that yet." Johnson once again tapped the phone against his hand. His posture remained tense, a sort of coiled anticipation making him appear ready for battle.

"Come on. Who else would do this?" Trent shoved both hands onto his hips.

"The better question is, where are the animals? Were they turned loose or stolen?"

Kara gasped and her hands flew to cover her mouth. "The festival is in two weeks! All the people who left their animals here after the hurricane. They're all gone? *All* of them?" It made no sense. Nothing pierced the fog of incomprehension. People were recovering from the hurricane. Every day, more had dropped by to retrieve the animals left in Trent's care until less than a dozen remained to be picked up.

But with the influx of strays brought in, litters of pups found in abandoned buildings and under piles of debris, the numbers of adoptable animals had soared to the peak of Forever Pals' capacity, even with the animals adopted out in the past months.

"One hundred and twenty-five animals." Trent muttered the number and rocked back on his heels. "If he took them, we may never find them. But he had to rent a boat to get them from here to the mainland. No way he took them to Mimosa. Too conspicuous. He'd need to disappear for a while."

"You're speculating." Johnson eyed Trent, the lines in his face growing taut.

"Meanwhile, you're not doing anything."

"Now look—"

Kara held up a hand to either of them. "Stop. Both of you. I don't know why you're fighting with each other, but it won't help us find those missing pets. Which should be our priority." She leveled a stare at Christian. "What do you need us to do?"

"Call the owners who still had pets here. Ask if any of their animals have shown up. I know some of those dogs, and if they were let loose to run the Islands, they'll go home. Call everyone you know and ask if they've seen any of the dogs you're missing." He tapped his phone and focused on Trent again. "I'll call my contacts in the city. Put them on the lookout for a possible fighting ring being set up and ask about a sudden influx of dogs for sale. If it is Snake, he won't be easy to find, but I won't let him get away with this."

Sarge woofed and rose to his feet, drawing Kara's attention to the German Shepherd she'd only then noticed. Animated, the dog strained forward, his nose directed toward the door.

"Too bad he flunked out of search and rescue. He might have been able to track Snake." Trent motioned at Sarge, and some of the strain lifted from his eyes.

"There's an idea. Tracking isn't the same as search and rescue." Deputy Johnson snapped his fingers and Sarge sat, then turned to face his handler. "If you had something of Snake's, he might sniff him out. But I can't ask him to find someone, or something, that he has no basic idea for. He's good, but it's not like I can say 'Find the dog' and Sarge knows what scent he's after."

Before Trent could snap a comeback, Kara prodded his side.

"We should start making phone calls and let Deputy Johnson get to work."

Trent traced the scar on his arm before jerking his hand away as though realizing the action drew attention not only to him but the past he shared with Snake. "Sure. Why don't you go home for the day? There's nothing else you can do here."

"Will you stop trying to get rid of me?" Kara wanted to comfort Trent. To reassure him that it didn't matter, and she had no fear about standing by his side. The words clogged her throat, locking together in a knot that tangled her tongue. She reached for his hand, drawing it into hers. "You start calling owners. I'll call Mel and the others."

Trent made a face like he'd tried to eat an entire bag of sour candy. Did he doubt her ability to make phone calls? Tugging her phone free, Kara tapped Mel's number first. The easiest to talk to, calling her first helped break the anxious tension already coiling across Kara's shoulders.

The animals needed her...needed all of them. She didn't have time to worry about whether she would mess up. *Deal with it later, Kara. Get the job done.*

At Mel's quick "hello", Kara paced the aisle and unloaded the last few minutes in verbal detail. Mel listened without interrupting, the occasional gasp punctuating Kara's speech. Promising to head out and begin looking, Mel disconnected, and Kara tapped the next person she knew who would jump at the chance to help. Darcy. Like Mel, Darcy held her questions, promised to begin looking, and hung up.

Kara cast a glance down the gray-green corridor in time to catch a glimpse of Trent as he disappeared into his office with his phone pressed to his ear.

Deputy Johnson had passed by during her conversation with Mel, his scowl intense.

Eying the list of contacts, Kara scrolled, looking for someone she knew well enough they'd accept her call and be willing to help. So many people flashed by. People she knew from church, from the shelter during volunteer days. But none she felt comfortable calling out of the blue.

The needs of the missing animals pressed hard against her chest, locking the fear and coldness into a hard lump. Crushing her eyes closed, she tapped the first number that rolled by. Becca Watson. A woman from church who Kara occasionally said hello to in passing at the grocery store and Sundays after church.

Kara's stomach tightened as the desire to end the call before Becca could answer flooded nervous energy through her limbs. When Becca answered, Kara blurted out her mission in a rush of breath, leaving herself on a gasp.

"You mean the whole shelter is empty and you think the animals are roaming around the Islands?" Becca's breath caught, and Kara heard the click of nails tapping a rapid beat. "Is one of them a little, runty-looking Labrador? Sort of a dingy white color, real standoffish?"

"Rex." Kara released the name while trotting toward Trent's office. "Where did you see him?"

"The crossroads between the churches. He's still there now. Should I grab him?"

"No." Her head shook side-to-side even though she knew Becca couldn't see. "He's one of our rehabilitation dogs. Non-violent, but if you approach, he might startle. I gotta go, Becca. We'll be right out."

Slapping the phone into her pocket, Kara burst into Trent's office and slid to a stop. He jerked forward in his chair, phone clutched to his ear and eyes popping wide.

Kara attempted a smile of reassurance, but from Trent's pinched expression, she failed. Rocking to her heels, she waited for him to wrap up the conversation, wincing at the high pitch emanating from the other side. After the ruckus a few weeks ago, today's calls might push people over the edge.

Trent gripped the phone while his knee popped up and down fast enough to rock the rolling chair back and forth. When the woman seemed to calm, Trent gave his apologies and hung up.

"Someone found Rex. If we hurry, we might be able to catch him before he roams any further." Words burst from her mouth, an excitement building that perhaps Snake hadn't stolen the dogs after all.

27

*T*rent shot up and snatched a leash from the wall as Kara bounced on the balls of her feet. Her joy pained him. He wanted to be optimistic, to believe they'd find all the animals safe and sound.

Standing on this side of the equation, nothing added up. A hundred dogs running across Hopper Island should have meant his phone was ringing off the hook with people wondering where the animals had come from.

Having Kara as the one excited and with an uplifted spirit while he resembled the Grinch on Christmas Eve left him off balance. Not that he'd ever traverse the many houses, taking away their hope and cheer, but his own had been sucked away. A hollowness grew within him, even as he hurried from the shelter and hopped into the truck without waiting to see if Kara kept up.

She did, slamming the truck door at the same time he cranked the engine. "I grabbed the food and his favorite toy." Waving the chewed-up rope in her hand, Kara clicked the seatbelt. "Let's check Life Walk first."

Right. He'd run out of the building without asking where the

159

dog had been spotted. "Got it." He clamped his jaw to keep from barking questions, to fill the sudden, tense silence radiating from the truck. Anything to keep from facing the fact he'd failed, again.

"This isn't your fault."

How she knew what he thought, he didn't know. Except, her ability to see into people and understand them had often surprised him. His scornful laugh had dissuaded harder people than her, but Kara merely tilted her head and hardened her jaw.

"Sorry."

"I don't need your apology. I need you to believe in yourself. You believe in me easily enough, thinking I could organize the adoption festival, but you're taking on the responsibility for Snake again." She scooped hair from her eyes before dropping her arm out the window.

Her palm beat a rhythm on the door in time with the slow pulse from the radio. Her calm demeanor soothed him, letting his chest expand in its first deep breath since he stepped into the empty shelter this morning.

"Why didn't you call me?" Kara shot a look his way, then waved away the question with a flapping palm. "Forget I said that. You had a million things on your mind. Well, a hundred and twenty-five, anyway."

Running his palms over the steering wheel as he made a turn toward the church, Trent allowed a grin to break through. "I had your number pulled up on my phone when Johnson arrived. After that, you showed up."

Trent swung into the church parking lot as Rex loped across the yard. The poor pooch limped, his right front paw leaving blots of crimson on the ground.

"Poor guy." Kara whispered despite Rex being unable to hear their voices from this distance. "I'll show him the food. Maybe he'll be willing to come back with us without a fuss."

He followed her toward the dog, keeping both in sight while remaining far enough back that Rex felt secure.

Rattling the bag of food, Kara whistled and called out. She carried herself forward with an easy gait, non-threatening and calm.

Rex stopped and swiveled in her direction, a low whimper bouncing across the lot. A few more steps, and Rex reached the end of his comfort zone. At his retreat, Kara froze and threw out her hand in a slashing motion that indicated Trent needed to follow her actions.

Trent had already stopped after seeing the fear in Rex's eyes. A person couldn't work in an animal shelter and not recognize the signs of a frightened animal unless they were completely oblivious. Following Kara's example, Trent sat down on the hard asphalt and lowered his hands to his knees. "Pour out some of the food. He's not starving. That'll make things harder, but maybe it will help him remember that we've been the ones feeding him for the last few months."

Rex lifted his ears at the sound of kibble hitting the ground. He sent a scorching look their way, once again the feral, fight-or-die stray they'd spent two weeks following around before they managed to gain his trust.

"What happened to you, Rex?" Trent patted his knee, drawing attention.

Ears shifting, Rex whined and hobbled forward one step, then another.

"We should call Kendall once we have him back at the shelter. That paw doesn't look good." Voice calm, eyes forward, Kara tossed a piece of food closer to Rex, who hopped on his three good legs to snatch up the morsel.

"How are things going with the festival?" Trent tossed a bite of kibble this time, drawing Rex even closer. They needed to keep talking, their attention on each other so Rex wouldn't feel threatened.

Kara rocked her hand back and forth in a so-so motion. "It's all coming together, thanks to Mel." She grimaced and slid her hands over her jean covered knees. Battered tennis shoes scraped across the pavement when she crossed her ankles. "Poor Mel. Planning a wedding, then I dump the festival on her. I wish…"

Her sigh tugged at him. "Wish what?"

"That I was braver." She tossed another bite, this one bringing Rex almost within reach. Smooching her lips together, Kara made a kissing motion that drew Rex and Trent's attention to her face.

A sort of agony slipped over him, compounded by the rush of feelings that overwhelmed everything else. "You are brave, Kara. Braver than I am."

"I keep telling you, don't say things you don't mean."

"And I keep reminding you, I do mean them. I'm not trying to flatter you. There's no reason for it. When I look at you, I see someone brave and resilient. You stood in front of a crowd and settled them down with words that cut straight to their hearts. That's where your strength lies. In your beliefs. In your heart." He reached for her, grazing his thumb along her jaw and over her ear, brushing hair away at the same time.

Rex edged into Trent's periphery, his long nose close to the ground as he sniffed out the pile of food.

Trent didn't move toward the dog. Kara held sway over him now.

If he did nothing else with the rush of feelings tangling together like a ball of Christmas lights, he needed Kara to understand how special she was. Not because of anything he believed, but because of who she was as a person. The woman God made and loved.

"I'll believe that when you stop taking on the burdens of everyone else's actions." She returned his stare, eyes bright and clear with emotions that looked as fierce and focused as his own.

Emotions neither of them seemed willing to name.

"Go out with me." He dropped his hand to her shoulder upon realizing the force of the plea had become lost to the demand of need. "Please. Will you go on a date with me?"

"Why?" Obvious confusion plucked her expression and sent her fingers dancing.

Her question corralled his racing thoughts. "Because when I'm with you, I'm better than I am on my own. You remind me of who I can be." *And I promised myself I wouldn't kiss you again until we were dating.* He held those words back by force of will, knowing they were too much. True, but too strong.

Rex whined and poked his cold nose into Trent's leg. Grinning at Kara, he slid the leash over Rex's neck and ran a slow hand over the dog's dirty back. "Come on. Let's get you back. Maybe Mel will have pity and give you a bath."

"I'll do it." Kara rose and brushed her hands over her rear, no doubt attempting to remove any dirt that dared lodge there. "Mel's out looking for more animals. Let me take care of him."

"I'll help you."

She lowered her eyes, rolled her shoulders, and lifted her head. "After the adoption, I'll go on a date with you. As much as I'd like to say yes and take off tomorrow, I can't. There's too much to do. Even with everyone helping." Kara spread her hands wide, the apology obvious.

"You don't have to explain. I'll help with that too."

"You need to be out there, looking."

"I can do both."

Kara grunted a mm-hmm and headed toward his truck.

Rex looked back at Trent, and the dog's eyes spoke volumes of how he felt. He'd chosen to trust again. Even after whatever actions had put him back on the street, the canine handed over his freedom without knowing what the future might hold.

163

Much like Trent needed to hand over his future to God instead of holding on, clutching the responsibility of others like anchors to his chest. *God, help me let go and be the man You made. Help me see my own value as You see me. And please, help Kara too.*

Following Kara, Trent patted his leg for Rex to join him, something the dog did without a second thought. Almost as though he understood that once the leash went around his neck, he became connected to—and protected by—someone who held his best interests at heart.

28

One week before the adoption day festival and Kara's list of things to do seemed to multiply instead of lessening.

Her map of the space showed vendors lining three sides, each lot taken by everything from Mel's grooming truck to Beth's food truck and Dermott with his plants. Using the parking lot at Forever Pals seemed easiest and gave Trent the ability to have all the animals close at hand. If they found the missing beasts in time.

First Mel's missing dog, now an entire shelter's inhabitants vanished. After Rex's retrieval, no others emerged from the Island's nooks and crannies.

Which led Trent to believe his old friend had stolen the animals and taken them to the mainland. What happened to them upon arrival, he could only speculate, but none of his admissions had given Kara a warm feeling.

Blowing her bangs from her eyes, Kara drew a precise checkmark beside the MUSIC notation on her checklist.

Trent stuck his head into the office, his perpetually tense frown never seeming to leave his face anymore, but his voice remained kind. "Christmas trees. What about a Christmas tree decorating contest? Winner gets a voucher for one of the venders. They'll each decide what the voucher offers and if they even want to participate."

"Where will we get the trees?"

"Leave that to me. I have a friend in the plant business." Trent started to back away, the gloom that had surrounded him darkening every encounter with anxious tension.

They needed to have a realistic conversation about the possibility of the dogs being gone for good. But she couldn't do that to him. Not now, when he resembled a kicked puppy. They'd agreed to proceed with the festival, even if the dogs were not found. Too many people had already agreed to come, and canceling the event seemed too much like conceding defeat. She refused to believe the animals were gone forever.

Kara pushed back from the desk and stretched to reach her pink hoodie. "We need decorations, and I know the place to find them."

"Need help?" For the first time in days, a light of something other than despair flicked through his eyes.

Kara bobbed her head, feeling like a bobble-head doll. "Your help and your truck."

"Your wish is my command." Keys jingled in the silence that cloaked the shelter.

Until the ominous lack of noise, she'd not realized how soothing the constant sound had been. With no scrabble of paws or yips, barks, or meows, the shelter closed in, the walls hovering and oppressive.

Kara shivered when they stepped from cold concrete to temperate wind.

"Where are we going?" Trent waited until after he pulled the truck into gear to pose the question she dreaded most.

"My parents' house." Rubbing her chilled fingers together, she cast a quick glance to gauge his mood. "They'll be the only ones home, so it won't be like that day after church. Granny lives in a small house across the drive, but she rarely comes to visit. Claims she paid her dues chasing her children and now it's their turn to hunt her down."

"I wasn't worried."

Based on the one-handed driving and smooth expression, Trent told the truth.

She offered directions, keeping the conversation to a minimum until the beach home came into view. Modest yet contemporary. Not a born and raised islander, she missed out on many of the early adventures and had to settle for stories of antics and mischief accomplished by Trent and the others during their younger years.

"Nice place."

"It's home." She shrugged, but the words resonated in her deepest heart. Her own cottage paled in comparison to this, a second home, but still comfortable.

No doubt hearing the truck's throaty rumble, her mother appeared from behind the house and approached, followed soon after by her father emerging from his workshop midway between the main cottage and Granny's one room tiny home.

If either parent were surprised, they hid it well. Mom wrapped Kara in a hug while Dad shook hands with Trent, then they traded places. Only after pleasantries were offered and accepted did her mom cock an eyebrow to ask what brought them out in the middle of a workday.

"Christmas." Kara shifted from foot to foot while wishing she spent the drive over preparing what she needed to say as succinctly as possible. "Trent had a great idea for the adoption day festival, and we need decorations. Lots of decorations."

Kara had to give her mom credit. She didn't jump and clap her hands. Instead, she placed her palms together in a pleading gesture. "You can have my decorations on one condition. Stay for dinner. Your dad and I will even help you sort everything and haul it wherever you're going."

"Mom, I really—" She caught Trent's eye, and the slightest dip of his chin that said he didn't mind. "Dinner sounds great."

"Hank, help Trent and Kara pull the boxes from the building. I'll start cooking."

"It's barely noon…how much are you planning to cook?"

"Don't ask." Her dad swished his hands through the air. "Paulette, I think a simple dinner will be fine. No need to keep them here all night." He winked at Kara, doing his best to placate the mothering instinct that would keep them elbow deep in boxes until her mom managed to call in the entire family for an impromptu dinner.

"We really don't have a lot of time." Kara insisted, pressing a tone of urgency into her voice. "One week until the festival isn't much. And there's so much to do."

"Let us help." Now Mom clapped and bounced.

Kara's stomach lurched. Did she dare tell her mother no? Saying yes meant the end of Kara's role in the project. Her mom couldn't resist taking over. Her genes orchestrated a dynamo of organization, spunk, and personality that Kara knew she'd never match. "I'm certain there's something you can help us with on adoption day." She tossed the crumb, praying it would be enough.

Trent leaned toward Kara and knocked his elbow into hers. "Kara has everything so perfectly organized I'm afraid to breathe on the papers. But there are loads of jobs that still need someone. Or you could be a judge in the decorating contest. We're using your decorations after all. Seems only fair."

Trent had no idea the can of worms he opened with that tease of authority.

Her mother ruled the roost of Christmas decorations and had a definite idea of planning and organization. Kara learned at her mother's knee, but the effervescent personality skipped on its merry way and left Kara lagging behind.

"I'd love to." Excitement blazed in Mom's countenance and brightened her cheeks to a rosy pink.

Dad nudged her toward the house. "It's settled then. You handle dinner. We'll tackle decorations."

"I'll call your brothers and let them know dinner's in a few hours."

"Mom. No. Please."

Her plea fell on deaf ears, her mother already waving to Granny, who stepped gingerly onto her front porch and shouted, "That the young man who stopped you at church?"

If Kara's face burned any hotter, her hair might ignite. Kara waved a hand in response, not trusting her voice since everything inside her felt mushy and wobbly as a newly set Jell-O.

Blowing out his cheeks with a sound like wind rippling through sails, her dad shook his head and gestured for them to follow. "Might as well get started. Sorry we couldn't head her off. You know how she loves to get everyone together."

Yeah. Too bad it always seems to end with me feeling like an idiot in front of my own family.

Kara kicked her feet through the short tufts of grass, feeling more like a pouting child with each step. Bringing Trent here had been a risk, but having her entire family descend on him... again? "You don't have to stay. I'll have Dad haul everything to the shelter."

"What makes you think I want to leave?"

His question drew her to a halt. He seemed relaxed, content even, to be here with her parents and the possible onslaught of siblings and a mouthy grandmother.

"Here we are." Her dad rolled open the old barn door, the wheels screeching with disuse. "Sorry about the mess. I've been reorganizing." He winked at Kara and disappeared into darkness barely broken by sunlight slanting through the open door.

"Don't tell your mother. She'll come down and mess up my system."

"System? Dad, you haven't had a system a day in your life."

"Exactly. And I like it that way."

Something clicked, and the barn filled with light. Kara gaped at the mountains of boxes, totes, containers, and a seemingly random mishmash she didn't want to investigate.

"Finally. Someone who understands my style and sense of order." Trent rubbed his hands together and approached a precarious stack of mismatched totes. "Let me guess. Christmas is in the boxes marked STUFF."

No way. Kara ping-ponged her gaze between them, watching in fascination as Trent hauled one box, then another, from the stack. Each one labeled with a hastily scrawled S and a blur of indecipherable characters and filled to the brim with garland, lights, ornaments, and the occasional tree topper.

29

*D*inner with Kara's family was an experience Trent couldn't wait to repeat. From the marvelous food her mother whipped up in a matter of hours to the raucous conversations bounding around the room, everything fit like a second skin.

Except Kara's silence.

And that no one seemed to notice she poked at her food and spoke in single syllables unless forced to compose full sentences.

It became the first month they'd worked together all over again.

He tried drawing her into the conversation and she seemed willing to join, until her brother spoke over Kara and pushed the conversation away from the festival and off to his deep-sea fishing adventures.

After that, Kara clammed up, her lips holding a thin line until he feared she might explode with repressed anger.

Once they left the house and slid back into his truck, she lowered her guard and relaxed into the seat with a long exhale. "Sorry."

"Not easy to be heard when everyone wants a chance to impress your parents."

"I guess." Kara pouted with a sweetness that broke his heart.

A need to be heard, to be listened to as though she mattered the way his dad listened to him pulsed in her crossed arms and locked jaw. She glared at the house. "You've no idea what it's like to never have anyone listen. To feel invisible. All the time."

"Is that why you freeze when you're asked to speak in front of a crowd? When you're used to disappearing into the background, it's not easy to step into the spotlight."

"You say that like you understand, but you don't. Not really. You didn't see what I saw in there. You're more comfortable with my family than I am. What does that say about me?" Her folded arms tightened, and she squeezed until white rings appeared across her nails.

Trent reached for her hand, tugging her across the seat until he could wrap an arm over her shoulders. "Your family loves you. I know it's hard to see sometimes. It took running away and coming back before I realized how much my dad loved me."

"I know. I love them too. It's so frustrating." Her hands flopped onto her lap and her hair drifted over his arm in a caress.

"Have you ever told them?"

"What would be the point?" She lifted her head and stared toward the beach house where her brothers spilled out onto the yard. "It's not them. It's me. My personality and the way I let myself get lost in the shuffle. It's why I struggle with this project, with forcing my ideas on other people. The last time I was put in charge of something like this was in seventh grade. It didn't go so well then and it isn't going well now."

"Excuse me but I think everything is going great." Trent squeezed her shoulder, pressing his thumb into the tense knot of muscle. "I believe in you. So do the others. We've loved your ideas. Especially the one about Christmas portraits."

"You're sure you don't need me at the adoption booth?"

"I know you'd rather take pictures. And we don't even have any animals to adopt since Snake took them. I can handle the booth. If things get crazy, all I have to do is shout." He took a deep breath. "What happens if we never find them?"

"Don't. Don't think like that. We'll find them. Or Johnson will. They'll be back." Her hands squeezed tighter in her lap. "I can't let myself think of what they're going through or the lives they'll live if they don't come back here."

Sliding away, Trent reached for the key and cranked the engine. "Let's get ready for next week."

Kara remained tight-lipped all through the rest of the evening as they organized and labeled boxes of ornaments and decorations. Each team would have a similar kit for their tree. What they did with it and the improvisations they added would be where the score came into play.

Through the next week, Trent paced, prayed, and paced more. The scar on his arm grew tender from the constant stroke of his fingers and his phone complained over the excess of calls by randomly shutting off or turning hot halfway through a conversation.

By the time Saturday morning rolled in, tension strung tightly enough to launch an arrow. Kara ran back and forth between the parking lot and the building, hauling boxes of decorations before the sun rose.

They passed each other countless times, each encounter drawing something from Trent he hesitated to acknowledge. Kara had hold of him with a fierceness he found surprising.

In a moment when she left the office with her arms full of seemingly random items, he stopped her with a hand on her arm. "Take a break."

"No time." She fidgeted as though uncertain, her feet tapping the floor.

Trent released her. Time later to say the things flooding his mind with images of Kara in a white gown walking down the aisle toward him. He'd already kissed her without a single date, why not imagine a marriage too?

He shook the thought away and twisted toward his office when the shrill ring of the shelter's phone blasted through the too quiet building.

Jerking the phone from the stand at the same time the answering machine clicked, Trent talked over his recorded voice. "Forever Pals animal shelter, this is Trent."

"Where've you been? Your man's been spotted. I need you to go with me. Bring all your paperwork on the stolen animals to verify what he has." Deputy Johnson's voice boomed loud enough Trent had to pull the phone away from his ear.

"You've found Snake?"

"That's what I said. I've been calling your cell since last night. Can't wait any longer. If you're not at the ferry by the time she leaves, you're gonna miss your chance to get those dogs back."

"I'm on my way. Don't let them leave without me." Trent slammed the phone down before Johnson could answer and bolted out the door calling Kara's name.

She answered him from the door, her eyes wide. "What's wrong?"

"I need you to take over for me today."

Right away, her head started to shake. Trent grabbed her arms, doing his best to keep the grip firm but not bruising. "They've found Snake. If I don't make the ferry, I'll lose all the animals. I have to go. I need you, Kara. Please."

She blinked at him, her lids moving slow enough to show the spidery blue veins crisscrossing the skin.

"I can't ask anyone else. You know this place, even better than I do. Talk to them the way you spoke to the group when they came for their pets. Connect with their hearts in a way I don't." He pulled her into a hug, willing his strength into her. "You can do this. I believe in you."

174

"Okay." Her whispered breath wavered, but her arms locked around his waist and her head rested for a single beat on his shoulder before she pulled back. "You better go if you want to catch the ferry."

I think I love you.

He couldn't tell her that. Not right now in the midst of the mess he'd allowed to swarm over her and consume the day she'd been working toward. This responsibility belonged on his shoulders. His actions put Kara in the spotlight, a place she could own if she allowed herself to believe and step out in faith.

A lesson she must learn for herself as he had to learn to let go of the pain caused by other people's actions.

Kara gave him a small push toward the door. "Go. Get the dogs back. And the cat. And don't forget the ferret."

Ferret. Right. Pulling the stack of papers that proved he had rights to the stolen animals, he flipped through, quickly counting folders, removing Rex's file, and tossing it onto the desk before leaving.

Out the door, he broke into a run, pelting the asphalt with pounding steps. Someone called his name, asking where he was running off to when the work was getting started. Sounded like Nigel, but Trent didn't pause to see. He trusted Kara to tell those who needed to know and smooth things over with the ones who didn't.

He rolled across the ferry dock as the final horn blasted. The man at the booth barely managed to wave him forward in time. Deputy Johnson waited beside his truck, dark sunglasses shading his eyes and a scowl becoming more obvious with each passing second. "By the skin of your teeth, man. Why didn't you answer your cell?"

Trent pulled the phone from his pocket, the screen once again black and silent. "Warranty must be up. It's been going crazy for the last few days." He powered it on, a flurry of notifications pinging at machine gun speed. His wallpaper flashed and went dark, the phone shutting off despite the little battery in the corner showing full power.

Shoving it back into his pocket, Trent shrugged. Ocean spray peppered his cheeks, the salty breath of wind carrying a tinge of hope.

30

*K*ara stood rooted to the spot where Trent left her, heart thudding hard enough to make her ribs ache.

Mel's face bobbed into view, but her words were lost to Kara's ringing ears. Only after shaking her head and pressing her fingers to her temples did the voice penetrate. "Kara, what's happened? Where's Trent?"

"They found the missing animals. Trent's gone to get them."

Mel whooped and threw her arms around Kara. "I knew it would all work out. Just when it seems hopeless, God makes a way."

I can't do this. God, help. Are You listening?

Ask God for help. That's what Trent said during one of their chats where she fell apart and he soothed the stress.

Mel's brows crinkled. "Are you okay? You look a little pale."

"I have to give Trent's speech." Why did her lips feel numb? Kara ran her tongue over her lip, feeling the familiar ridges.

"I could—" Mel's elbow in Zeke's gut stopped whatever else he might have said. An invitation to take Trent's place, probably.

Kara found her head shaking without her approval. She had

to do this. To prove once and for all that when the chips were down, she was not a friend who left someone hanging.

Her phone alarm rang, startling Kara from her reverie. Time to begin the festival. The tables were in place, decorations ready. The mobile businesses lined one side of the parking lot, banners waving and the scent of something wonderful drifting from Beth's booth.

Trent's Christmas trees took up one side of the building, each one perfectly balanced in a tree stand, their green branches emitting the most appealing scent of all.

The scent flooded her system, working away the worry.

Please, help me. Lord, I believe You can.

Purpose filled her mind while peace flooded her heart and eased the tight clutch of panic bubbling and churning her stomach. "I need all the vendors to gather here." Kara motioned toward the adoption booth draped in red and green with sprigs of holly tucked into the folds.

"I'll tell everyone on the far side of the lot." Mel dashed away, Zeke trailing behind with a ghost of a smile.

Kara motioned toward the long row of friends working on their tables and booths. Leaving their stalls to crowd close, they appeared ready and eager to accept her as leader for a day.

"First of all, on behalf of Forever Pals, I want to thank all of you for coming. Your support means the world to Trent and me, and even though he can't be here right now, I know he'd want you to know how honored he is by your willingness to join us so close to Christmas. If you have any questions, I'll be here." Drawing a deep breath, Kara willed her expression to remain open and friendly instead of becoming hard and cold.

"Where is Trent?" Mallory spoke up from the back of the crowd, a tote full of books slung across her shoulder.

"He's away on an errand but should be back soon." Kara deflected. A low murmur started, a general feeling of unhappiness spreading through the gathering of entrepreneurs. "Okay, look." She spread her hands out, ignoring the chill of her fingers and shaking hands. "You all know the animals were stolen. We considered stopping the festival. After all, what's an adoption day festival without the adoption?"

Their eyes widened, colors of every shade seemingly locked onto Kara's face and drawing the breath from her lungs. She pushed on, a wordless prayer flitting through her mind. "But this day isn't just about Forever Pals. This is for you too. The first annual Hopper Christmas Festival. I pray it's the first of many and that all of you have a wonderful day of fellowship, friendship, and of course, sales."

A roar began in the back, near Mallory, the voice too deep to belong to the feisty bookkeeper. Soon, the others joined in, belting out "Joy to the World" with surprising harmony.

Tucking her shaking hands into her pockets, Kara eased back toward her table. "The first customers will be arriving any minute."

Taking that as their dismissal, the group scattered amid a general cacophony of laughter and shouting. Zeke wrapped an arm around Mel, pulling her close for a peck on the cheek. Mel's face glowed, the love appearing quick as a wink when she stared up at her adoring husband.

Kara didn't bother holding back the grin at their adorable newlywed antics. Although her parents still acted the same way on occasion.

"What can we do to help?" Beth, Pen, Scott, and the majority of the mobile business owners crowded close to Kara's table.

"I need someone to make certain the signs to the bathrooms are clearly labeled and the other doors locked. Even though the building is empty, we don't need people wandering around in there." Kara pointed her chin at the glass door where most of Forever Pals traffic moved in and out.

Mindy gave a thumbs-up and left the table.

"Beth, you're the only food vendor and I'm sure you'll be

swamped. Do you have someone who can run errands for you? I know you have extra supplies stored in the kitchen here. I'll need to give them a key to get in and out through the side door. Make certain they lock the door behind them every time they leave. It'll be a pain, but we can't afford anyone getting inside who isn't meant to be there."

"Scott will help." Beth patted Scott's arm, and something flashed between them.

Kara passed Scott the key and moved on. "The Christmas tree decoration contest is one of the last events of the evening. We have judges already, but what I need are people who can help move boxes out of the way and keep the paths clear between tables."

Three people raised their hands. Kara gave them a nod of appreciation. "When Trent returns, hopefully with the animals in tow, we'll need help moving the dogs from the truck to the building. We don't know what sort of shape they'll be in, so I might need Kendall on standby. They won't return today, but God willing, soon."

"He's found them?" Abby spoke up, her head barely breaking even with the shoulders around her.

"We think so. I'm sorry, I should have mentioned that earlier. Trent had to leave Hopper to follow up on a lead with Deputy Johnson from Mimosa's police department." The nervous energy reappeared, sapping the warmth from her fingers and toes and pooling it in her face. "That's all for now. When anyone has a free moment, I would appreciate if you made a quick round through the tables to check on the others. Some only have one person manning the booth. We all know how stressful that can be. Offer to take over and let them stretch their legs, grab something to drink, or use the restrooms."

They drifted away again, this time their pace slower and faces lit with a mixture of excitement and compassion. Like children on Christmas morning, the anticipation swelled to audible levels. The band tuned instruments from the makeshift stage at the entrance and soon the air filled with cheery tunes.

Another buzz from her phone alarm and Kara waved to Cooper who manned the iron gate entrance where a line of people gathered. The initial rush of chatter drowned out the band before people scattered like fish after someone slapped the water.

Deep breath. Smile.

A woman approached Kara's table and lifted one of the pamphlets. Remus and Romulus smiled back from the front cover, their doggy expressions able to break through even the hardest hearts. "Are these two available?"

Kara nodded even though her heart sank. The twin huskies might be the only dogs adopted today unless Trent pulled off a miracle. But without him here, Kara didn't have the manpower to let the woman spend time with either dog.

"Those two are young, barely a year old. They're lovely dogs, but I will warn you that they have incredible amounts of energy. Can I ask what type of pet you're hoping to find?" She folded her hands, thankful for the steady cadence in her voice.

"My grandson wants a puppy for Christmas. His parents don't approve. But if I give him one anyway, they'll have to keep it." The glee in her voice and the way her red nails scraped over the photo drew Kara's spine into a ramrod straight line.

"I'm pleased you're thinking of adopting. How old is your grandson?"

"Three. And his mother is seven months pregnant with a little girl."

Good Heavens. No wonder the parents didn't want a puppy. "If I might be so bold, perhaps a stuffed animal would suffice for a pet this year. That's quite a bit of responsibility." Kara motioned toward the table where her grandmother's crocheted items rested in bold reds and cheery yellows, the crocheted animals a huge hit with most crowds. "There are a few possibilities there, if you'd like to take a look."

The woman followed Kara's direction, taking the pamphlet with her.

Whew. First customer and disaster averted. Kara attempted to relax. The day had only begun, and she couldn't afford to spend all her energy on one person.

*I*n the heart of a series of derelict and abandoned buildings set to the side of garbage littered streets and covered in graffiti, Trent walked into a horror show of depravation.

Anger lodged, fast and firm, the heat of it burning away the fear. Johnson held out a hand for Trent to wait. Police made their way through the building, intent on their targets.

"Look who's here." Snake slithered forward, unconcerned with the uniformed men.

Trent shoved aside Christian's hand and crossed to where Snake stood with a leash in one hand and a bottle in the other. The dog—a lean mastiff Trent knew as Toby—cowered at the end of the tether.

"You've gone too far this time." Trent reached for the leash, ripping it from Snake's hand.

Sloshing liquid over his chest, Snake hissed a curse. His slurred words dragged with painful memories. "This what it takes to bring you back?"

"I'm not back." Trent backed away, and the dog followed.

"I'm sorry for all the trouble I caused you, but I'll never regret leaving."

Snake threw the glass bottle, shattering it against an exposed metal beam before he rushed Trent. Death and hatred flared in his black eyes.

Deputy Johnson stepped in, his body blocking Snake. More men moved through the warehouse, Kevlar vests winking in and out of the muted glow of dirty bulbs.

Dogs whined, their combined voices drawing Trent toward a heavy black door off to the side. While the police officers scoured the building for men, Trent only wanted the animals he'd lost. The heart and soul behind his business and the only thing he cared about right here and now.

They needed him. Unlike the first time when he gave them a loving home and place to be safe, now they needed him to soothe away the fear and possible unfortunate wounds of fighting for a loveless man who saw money as the worthwhile thing in life.

Opening the door took Trent from destitute to bottom-of-the-dumpster despair. In cages too small for even a cat to find comfortable, his dogs whined. Battle-scarred and weary, their tails thumped the cage walls. Many of them set up a chorus of reproach, the tone begging for salvation and threatening to drop Trent to his knees.

How had he ever done this to a living animal? Not to this level, but his sin of cruelty had been no less agonizing.

He reached for the latch of the first cage, stopping when Johnson's forceful grasp clamped on his wrist. "Paperwork first. The trucks are here. Show proof of ownership, let the men get evidence, and you can have them back. But if you open that cage now, you risk undermining the entire operation."

A bluff. It had to be a bluff. Trent tightened his grip. The tiny mixed breed trapped inside eyed him with a mixture of hope and fear. He released the latch and stepped back, unable to condemn a single animal to a future outside his control.

Trent faced the dog, listening to its cries for freedom, and felt his own heart respond. Hadn't he been in this terrible cage for years? A cage of his own creation. A latch made by his own hand. God opened the door for him when he walked away from this life.

But he'd been too afraid to move. Locked in anger and grief over his past, he'd cowered as the dog did, hunched in pain and disbelief of rescue. Of worthiness.

Trent passed the leash to Johnson. "I never told you I was sorry for breaking into your house all those years ago. I apologized to your dad because I had to, but I never thought of how it made you feel to have your home become tainted by bad memories."

Johnson shrugged, but a sadness lingered in his eyes. "I looked up to you. You probably never knew that. We were in different classes, but I always saw you around. Camp or whatever. That night changed all that. You'd become someone else, someone sinister and broken. You violated my trust, even though you never realized you had it."

"I'm sorry."

"Until that night, I always thought I'd be something other than a cop. After all the years of hearing Dad's stories, I wanted no part of that life. But after you were taken away and I learned you'd left for the city, I knew. I had to take a stand. Be the hedge between the innocent and those who yearned to break through from the other side." Johnson smiled a grim smile, the look almost gruesome in the odd light. "I became a cop because of you. I should thank you for that, even though I had nightmares for years."

"If I could take it back, I would. In a heartbeat." Shame pierced, poised to hold the knife edge to Trent's throat for the rest of his life. How could he ever recover from this blow? From knowing the depth of pain he'd caused.

Before, it appeared as some dark shadow, a lingering presence he brushed away with good deeds and apologies. Now it surrounded, suffocating with a nauseating stench.

"We all make our own choices, Trent. You made yours and I made mine. Sure, your decisions affected me, but I chose my path. At any time in the last ten years, I could have changed it, left the job, and become something else. But I love what I do." Christian shrugged and reached down to pat Toby's back. The dog leaned against Johnson's leg, his tongue darting out to swipe the gentle hand. "My actions are my own."

"People keep telling me that."

"Maybe it's time you listen."

Someone called for Johnson, a black-vested man who stood in the doorway and glared. "There's more you need to see."

Trent's heart thumped at the darkness in the tone. "How long until I can take my animals home?"

The man shrugged broad shoulders. "Can't answer that. Not yet. Stick around though. We need as many professionally trained people as we can get. Animal control is outside, waiting. They'll do a general wellness check before we start moving them."

A woman with a camera breezed past the man, reminding Trent of Kara.

He glanced at his phone and groaned. Still dead. He'd tried multiple times to power it on, but nothing worked.

No way he'd make it back in time for the festival. All those potential adopters waiting for animals. Drumming his fingers across the phone's casing, an idea formed. "Can I take pictures too? That way I can compare them with my paperwork while I wait. Not all these dogs are mine. I'd be willing to take them." He hurried to reassure the harried cop whose lips had thinned to a flat line. "But I want to make certain all of mine are accounted for. We'll work out the particulars on the rest later. They might be missing pets too."

"Go ahead." Johnson made a waving motion with his hand. He passed his cell phone to Trent and motioned for the man to move ahead. The cops disappeared into some unknown corner of the building, leaving Trent with the photographer snapping pictures in rapid-fire succession.

Trent joined her, lifting the borrowed phone for picture after picture. They didn't have Kara's flair or beauty. These photos were raw, heart-wrenching in their unglorified dignity.

"You're the one these guys were stolen from?" The photographer held the camera to her eye and clicked before thrusting out her hand. "Nicole."

"Trent." He shook the offered hand. "You take pictures like this often?"

"This? Nah. Crime scene photography can be a bit gruesome. This is heartbreaking, but with a happy ending." She managed a smile while nodding toward one of the more outgoing dogs who pressed his snout against the bars and wiggled for attention. "Happy endings are what give me the strength to keep going."

Happy endings.

Did he have a happy ending out there somewhere? Apologies given. Actions granted an undeserved reprieve. God's grace covered it all.

Trent rolled his shoulders and began tapping the screen, grateful he'd memorized Kara's number as he sent image after image to her with a caption for help. These animals needed him. Needed them. The people at the festival. The shelter. The love and commitment of a stable home.

Sending the last picture, Trent hovered between rows of cages. Trapped in place physically while he took a spiritual step out of the self-made cell and into the dawn of a new lease on life.

God, I don't want to hide anymore. Help me leave this cage of doubt and fear. You've thrown open the door. Give me the courage I need to leave and never return.

The first breath filled his lungs with sour refuse. But the second. On that breath, he smelled the fresh gleam of freedom. A new life. One where he held himself responsible for his actions and accountable for his life while knowing the joy of the Lord.

I want to go home again.

32

*K*ara slid her hand into her pocket, checking her phone for the hundredth time for news from Trent. She forgave the first hour of silence since the ferry took that time. But the three hours since then—without even a single note to say they'd arrived safely—began to wear on her ability to focus on the stack of applications filled out and waiting for approval. They needed animals ready to adopt first.

A single yelp drew Kara's attention away from the paperwork and over to the crowd building in front of Beth's cookie decorating booth.

Cooper held a woman's arm, the same woman he'd rescued from the parrot. She flashed a bright smile in Cooper's direction before bending down to retrieve her fallen cookie from the pavement.

Kara's phone pinged, then began a rapid beeping of incoming messages dropping in so fast her phone seemed to vibrate with energy. Curious, she drew the slim case from her pocket and tapped the messages from Christian while her heart took up new lodging in her throat.

Dogs of every shape and size took over her screen. Kara fell

189

back, landing hard on the camp chair. She knew these dogs. Lucky. Delilah. Sadie. They were all there. Relief clutched her breath, shortening it into tight bursts.

The strum of a guitar drew her eyes to the stage. Everyone needed to know that Trent had succeeded. Their animals would soon return to the Island and then to their loving arms. Those who hadn't yet found a home—she eyed the stack of applications—the possibilities were endless.

Everywhere she looked, people browsed the stalls. Many walked away with their arms filled and smiles on their faces. Carts. They needed little carts or wagons for the shoppers to haul their purchases around in. Kara tapped out a note to herself for next year's festival and leaned forward to settle her elbows on the table.

Zeke's sister Abby worked the photography booth, showing remarkable instinct for lighting and with enough natural enthu-siasm to comfort even the fussiest baby whose parents had seemed to give up on him quieting long enough for a quick picture. Their joyful exclamations reached Kara at the same time Mel popped over for one of her "How you doing?" moments.

This time, Kara had work for the other woman. She passed Mel the phone. "Can you print out a few of these? Use the template for lost pets but change it to fit what we're doing today. I have an idea."

To Mel's credit, despite the questions no doubt bubbling through her head, she took the phone and dashed toward the building.

Scott strolled from the kitchen entrance, taking Beth another batch of something or other.

Kara's stomach rumbled. After the sudden release of tension, her system reminded her no food had been given today.

"Need anything?" Another man Kara didn't recognize paused in front of her table. "I've left Sam in charge and thought

I'd take a turn around the booths. Sam wanted one of Beth's cookies. Can I get you one too?"

"That would be great. Thanks." No sense denying the gnawing in her midsection. Not when satisfying it meant one of Beth's famous cookies. Didn't matter which recipe she used today, Kara had every bit of faith that it would be wonderful. Her stomach gave an anticipatory growl that the man thankfully couldn't hear as he walked away.

Mel and Kara's cookie arrived simultaneously, and Kara scooted the napkin closer while thanking Max, the name provided courtesy of Mel when she returned and said hello.

Kara shifted her attention away from the flyers. What she was about to do required something in her stomach other than coffee.

When Mel hesitated, her hands folding together then unfolding in succession, Kara lifted her head as Mel's question seemed to launch out. "Trent really found them? Is he bringing them back?"

"Yes. And as far as I know, yes. There's some legal stuff to do first. No idea how long it will take."

The relief cascading over Mel's face matched the salsa of Kara's own pulse. Sweet and warm, the bite of cookie slid down her throat and eased the tightening cramp of apprehension. "I'm going to make an announcement soon. Would you help me gather everyone in front of the stage?"

"Sure." Mel motioned toward the sweet treat. "When you're ready, give me a wave."

Kara saluted and took another bite. The band struck up another tune, this one a song Kara knew but couldn't place until the first words dropped from the singer's lips. "Mary Did You Know" had always been a favorite. Hearing it now, really listening to the story and letting the words work through to her soul, tears gathered in the corners of her eyes.

What would that be like? To know your child's future would

be filled with pain and a too-early death. At least from a mother's perspective. From the side of the Savior, His death was perfectly timed and freely given.

If He could do that for her, the least she could do was take the blessing and make the most of her Christian walk. To use her voice for the pets begging for help.

God. I'm not worthy to be one of Yours. But I suppose no one is. Your Son was perfect. Help me to be more like Him.

Kara lifted her head and straightened her shoulders. Dropping a sign on the table, she wove through the crowd and waved at Mel, who nodded and began an earnest conversation with Zeke. They split, and the surrounding people started making their way toward the stage.

Stopping at the steps, Kara motioned to the music coordinator and whispered her plea into his listening ear.

He nodded and squeezed her arm. When the band finished their song, he strolled up the steps and slid a hand in front of the microphone while talking with the singer whose voice could melt butter in Antarctica.

The singer motioned Kara onto the stage. "Ladies and gentlemen, we have an announcement from Kara, our event coordinator for today's festivities. Give her a round of applause, then listen close because she has some important information for you."

She expected polite clapping, so when the crowd generated an ear-stopping pounding, Kara blushed and waved a hand at them. The sudden smile felt genuine, and her body relaxed as she focused on one face after another. To look at all of them, to even consider the mass huddled before her incited panic. But one at a time, from friend to friend, Kara let the words form in her heart and fall from her lips.

"As most of you know, the shelter's animals were stolen a few weeks ago. Trent left this morning on a mission to retrieve them. He's sent me a message, the animals have been found, but they're in bad shape." The heavy gasps forced Kara to pause and wipe a tear away before she continued. "Mel, would you pass out the flyers?"

Mel and Zeke circled through the crowd, handing out the papers Mel had printed. Many of the women clutched the papers in their hands while the men's faces showed anger as their jaws tensed and arms crossed.

Knowing the anger was directed toward the people responsible and not toward her, Kara drew a deep breath. "The picture you see is a young dog, whose name is Tex. Named for the Texas shaped mark on his ribs, which you can hardly see because he's become so emaciated in the weeks he's been away from us. I know many of you came here today with the hopes of seeing the dogs, playing with puppies, and maybe even taking one home. That's the goal of Forever Pals, to connect you with a pet who will become a lifelong companion."

Heads began nodding. Mel, Sam, and Abby beamed smiles in Kara's direction.

"A pet is a responsibility. They deserve love and care. Not this. Christmas is upon us. A time of love and goodwill. I'm not asking you for money. I'm asking for something else. Something more important..."

She paused, letting the mood settle and sink in.

"Understanding. That's what Forever Pals needs from you now. These dogs will be traumatized and need rehabilitation. I'm asking you to give them grace and give us time to work with them. To help them become the pets you've dreamed of."

Kara stopped amid boot-stomping cheers and shouts. Someone whistled, the sound slicing through the noise. Others took up a cadence by clapping, and the band dipped into "It's the Most Wonderful Time of the Year" amid another round of cheers.

Mel rushed to the steps, clasping her hands beneath her chin and a huge smile on her face. "That was amazing! I'm so proud of you." She threw her arms around Kara when she drew close enough, nearly crushing her ribs with the embrace.

Kara beamed. It was amazing. Not because of what she did, but because of the peace she felt about it. No tumbling thoughts as she replayed every word, worrying over whether anything she said had sounded stupid or disjointed. Simple, beautiful peace.

Her mother waved from the back of the parking lot, sunlight bouncing off her blonde curls. She pressed both hands to her lips and threw them out in wide arcs—a shower of kisses and praise that settled deep into Kara's heart.

33

*E*xhausted, downhearted, and unable to string more than one thought together at a time, Trent parked the truck in the Forever Pals parking lot and leaned his forehead against the steering wheel.

Three days he'd been battling red tape while the deputies rounded up Snake and his cronies. Photos of the stolen dogs, combined with his records showed a clear path of ownership, but the detectives needed to make sure they had everything before releasing the animals to Trent's care. Animals so exhausted they'd barely made a sound during the ride home.

Three days away from Kara and the Islands Trent loved. And now that he'd returned, how many more days would the dogs be punished with unresponsive adopters and a general feeling of distrust?

After dealing with the hurricane and Trent's failure, how much goodwill did the residents of Hopper have left?

I can't do this alone.

Someone pecked on his window, the ping of a fingernail giving him the instant perspective the person waiting for him was female. His heart stuttered a beat. Who would be waiting for him here, now? No one knew to expect him except Kara. He'd sent her a late-night text saying he'd be on the morning ferry before he buckled in for one last night in a cheap motel.

Another peck, the rat-a-tat showing a hint of impatience.

Trent lifted his head and found Kara beaming at him in the early morning fog. Wrapped in a wooly sweater with her hands tucked into the sleeves after she knew she'd caught his attention, she jerked her head toward the building.

Trent rolled down the window. "What are you doing here?"

"And a good morning to you too." Kara hopped from foot to foot, drawing his attention to her slippered feet. The woman wore slippers shaped like huskies, complete with ears and tails.

"Sorry."

"Don't apologize. You're tired and cranky. What do you want to do first? The kennels are ready, but you look like you could use some coffee and a hearty breakfast." She shivered.

"I'll eat later. Let's get them inside…after you put on some real shoes."

Kara wiggled her toes and grinned at him again. How could she smile right now? The show of gladness seemed beyond him. Not that he wasn't happy to be back and have every single missing animal with him, but the sheer magnitude of the upcoming weeks landed on his body with a resounding thud that felt remarkably like handcuffs.

"Come inside with me while I change shoes." She pulled his door open and snagged his sleeve.

"I'll go ahead and bring in the first few dogs while you do that. We need to get them out of these cages."

"Trent Raines, get inside the shelter right now." She pointed, even stomped her foot for good measure, though it only made him want to chuckle. "You have all the help you need."

People flooded from all corners of the building with leashes in hand and smiles splitting their faces.

"No, Kara. They can't. The dogs are frightened. They might

get hurt." He started forward, intent on heading off the volunteers.

"Trust us. This one time, let go and trust that someone else can help." Kara wrapped an arm around his waist, the contact taking the sting out of her words. "I've been training them on what to do. If anyone feels uncertain, they'll wait. You need rest."

"Johnson called, didn't he?"

Kara merely shrugged at his statement. "He was worried about you. Said you wouldn't sleep until they were back."

"I slept…a little." He clarified when Kara rolled her eyes.

Mel lowered the ramp on the truck and hurried inside.

Trent started to follow.

Kara released him, and the loss of contact stopped him in his tracks.

Trust.

Mel reappeared, a small terrier mix in her arms. The dog whined and licked her chin, the thin tail smacking Mel's arm with each pass.

Zeke went next, bringing out a large mastiff on the end of his leash. Like the terrier, this dog appeared thrilled to be walking alongside a stranger.

"Come on." Holding Kara's hand, Trent led them into the building and to his office, where he closed the door. A look around showed the office transformed from his untidy, cramped space to an even more crowded sleeping room. An air mattress rested against the wall, the coverings and blankets tossed haphazardly across his one good chair. "Who's been sleeping here?"

A laugh shot out from Kara, startling them both as she clapped a hand over her mouth. "You sound like Papa Bear from *Goldilocks*." Her giggle untied the knots in his stomach. "After the festival, I brought a few things over. I knew you might show up anytime, and I wanted to be here." Kicking off her slippers and shoving her feet into a pair of beat-up sneakers, Kara pointed at the coffeemaker. "Coffee's fresh."

"I need something else. Three days of nothing but coffee." Trent grimaced at Kara's back when she turned and snagged a bar of some sort from her backpack.

"Eat this then, if you won't do anything else. The protein will be good for you."

Still not what he wanted. How did he tell her without scaring her away? Any woman in her right mind would run away from someone with a past like his. *A forgiven past, Trent. Remember that.*

"Kara." Trent pulled Kara close and let his eyes close as a long breath leaked out. "I missed you."

"I think you mean that." Holding him close, Kara rested her head against his chest. "'Bout time for a date, don't you think?"

"I'll say." He waited a beat before sliding a hand around to press against the back of her head. "Maybe even two or three."

"You should know, we have pledges for every animal in that truck."

Shock rendered him speechless, and his arms relaxed their tight hold.

"They need your final approval, of course, but on first look, they're all wonderful homes. And they're willing to wait until the dogs are ready." Kara took a step back, uncertain perhaps what his silence meant.

"When did this happen?"

"At the festival." Kara blushed as pretty as a morning sunrise, the pink in her sweater matching her cheeks. "I reminded everyone how animals love us."

He could see her, confronting everyone with determination and grace. Her passion breaking over her face and lighting the world with a sense of justice and purpose.

"They leave a mark."

"Footprints." Kara sighed and relaxed into his arms when he

198

pulled her close again. "They leave footprints on our hearts. As you have on mine."

A joke landed on the tip of his tongue, something blasé and trite. He ignored it and reveled in Kara's arms around his waist.

Perhaps one day, she might grow to love him.

Until then, this was enough. To know she held some part of him in her heart. He'd made a difference in her life, as she had in his.

Now he had to figure out how to make it snow.

THE END

ABOUT THE AUTHOR

Tabitha Bouldin is a member of American Christian Fiction Writers (ACFW) and an avid reader. When she's not busy home-schooling her two boys, you'll find her buried in a book.

facebook.com/tabithabouldinauthor

twitter.com/tabithabouldin

instagram.com/tabithabouldin

goodreads.com/tabithabouldin

pinterest.com/tabbycat38585

bookbub.com/authors/tabitha-bouldin

ALSO BY TABITHA BOULDIN

The Trials Series
Trial by Courage
Trial by Faith
Trial by Patience

Standalone novels and novellas
Macy's Dream
Christmas in Jingle Junction
Wish Upon a Star

Independence Islands:
Mishaps Off the Mainland
Stealing the First Mate

BOOKS IN THE HOOPER ISLAND SERIES

Flipping Hearts (Book One) by Chautona Havig

Seasoned Grace (Book Two) by Melissa Wardwell

More Than a Heartthrob (Book Three) by Kari Trumbo

Hooper Safe Haven (Book Four) by Rachel Skatvold

Footprints on Her Heart (Book Five) by Tabitha Bouldin

Reclaiming Hope (Book Six) by Carolyn Miller

RECLAIMING HOPE

HOOPER ISLAND BOOK SIX SNEAK PEEK

CAROLYN MILLER

*C*heck, check, check, check, check! Was anything more satisfying than checking off items on a list and seeing just how productive one had been? Perhaps the only thing more satisfying might be when one added things to the list only to check that off immediately too, Callie Steele thought, smiling to herself as she finished up Greener Gardens' to-do list for the day.

"Callie, you're still here?" Samantha Green—no, Sam Fairhaven now—said as she entered the office. "I knew it was a good day when you said yes to working here, but I didn't expect you to live in the office."

"It's only just after six," protested Callie.

"Try nearly seven," countered Sam. "The only reason I stopped in was because I saw the light on as we were passing."

"Is Max with you?"

"He's in the car. He knew I'd have some fun trying to get you to quit work for the day. Workaholic was the term used, I believe."

She felt it only right to protest. "I like working."

"And you're very good at it and have been such a blessing to me and Max, as you very well know. But neither of us wants to see you burning out just because you enjoy work so much. So go on. Go home."

"Is that an order?"

"Yes," Sam said, but within the tease Callie recognized her employer's concern. "You are hereby being ordered to go home, put your feet up, and watch something dreadful on the telly."

"Dreadful on the telly?" A chuckle escaped. "Now look who is being influenced by a certain half English personage who shall not be named."

Sam laughed, but held the door open. "Max said he's coming in here if you're not out in five."

"Fine. You don't need to send in the heavies." Although Max could never be accused of that. Sam's new husband was as fit and kind as the day Callie had first met him over a decade ago. He hadn't always been. His first wife's death had shattered him to reclusive rudeness, and it was only through finding love with Sam that he'd mellowed into the charming man who now wrote novels with a happy ending.

If only such fairy tales existed for all.

Callie saved her work and collected several files to deal with later at home.

"Ahem."

At Sam's raised brows, she put them back. "I can't believe you don't want me to get this done. I could finish it tonight."

"You know what I want? For you, my dear friend, to relax, to enjoy life for once, make the most of this beautiful August weather, instead of running around looking after us all the time."

"But—"

"Go."

"Fine." Callie pasted a smile on her face and moved past Sam, down the three steps, and outside. Behind her, she could hear Sam locking up. Beyond her, Max Fairhaven, famous novelist, sat in his red sports car, smirking at her like he knew what she was thinking.

She shrugged, turning her back on him. She'd be working for him again tomorrow morning, and between now and then would be plenty of time to sit on her own, by her lonely self, eating dinner for one, thinking of a smart comeback to her boss and his usual espousal that she should find a man.

Like he actually believed there were available single Christian men of appropriate age and education and shared interests hanging around on trees.

Maybe there were. Just not on any of the Independence Islands' trees she'd ever seen.

Callie waved as Sam climbed into the sports car, watching as they pulled away, then moved through the plants between the office and the house. After her marriage, Sam had let Callie use the Greens' former home, and Callie appreciated having the extra space. But truth be told, it was a little lonely coming here. Work filled the silence, kept the angst at bay, helped numb the doubts and questions.

She unlocked the back door and met with a flash of fur and a protesting meow.

"Sorry, Adam." Callie bent to pat the tabby, a recent gift from her mother, which Callie chose to believe was *not* a sign of things to come. Even if her mother seemed to have given up hope that Callie would find a man with her comment that, "A cat will at least provide some company for you."

Thanks, Mom. She moved to the kitchen, shoulders slumping at the leftover remains in the fridge. Tired salad. Half a bowl of brown rice. Leftover curry with way too many lentils. Boring, boring, boring.

Indicative of her life. Boring, boring, boring.

Another protest from Adam. She grabbed his can of meat and scooped tonight's portion into his bowl. "At least there is one male in this world who loves me," she murmured.

He glanced up at her then buried his face in his bowl again, ignoring her as was his wont.

Okay, so maybe the thought that Adam loved her held more hope than reality.

Another glance at the fridge showed the contents hadn't changed. Maybe she should shake off this funk and go out to get something to eat.

Fifteen minutes later, she pulled up outside Granny Mae's, the Victorian building in the main part of town that housed one of the few places that was open for dinner tonight.

Inside, she was relieved to not see Max and Sam, relieved to not see anyone she knew. Who wanted to advertise one's lone diner status? But it seemed there were no spare tables.

"I'm so sorry, Callie," Kelly, the middle-aged waitress said. "I thought we had room, but it seems I miscalculated. I could see if the gentleman over there will share with you."

Callie glanced in the direction she pointed. The dark-haired man was dressed in business attire, smooth, groomed—totally her thing. Unlike the man seated at a table nearby, whose scruffy, sun-streaked hair almost hit his shoulders as he talked with an older couple, his tanned skin gleaming under the light. Imagine the skin damage...

"Wait here."

"Oh, but—"

Kelly hurried off before Callie could finish her objection and went to speak to the man. He looked up, then glanced in Callie's direction, shrugged.

She summoned a small smile. He looked to be younger than her, in his late twenties. She followed Kelly's gesture to move closer and stood by the table. "Hi. Thank you."

His gaze swept up and down, then he shrugged again and shoved the last of his burger inside his mouth.

She took that as acquiescence and slid awkwardly into the booth. A quick scan of the menu Kelly handed her and she ordered, Kelly left, and Callie glanced apologetically at the man again. "Thanks again. I really didn't mean to interrupt you."

His eyes narrowed. "Then I don't understand why you're here."

She blinked. "I beg your pardon?"

"You say you don't want to intrude, yet here you are." He swallowed the dregs of his drink. "I bet you're one of those women who think you're entitled to do what you want because you're middle-aged."

What? Shock dragged her jaw to the table. He might dress to impress, but his manners were so uncouth.

"And here is your drink, Callie."

She swallowed past the sting still lodged in her throat to murmur a thanks.

"Is everything okay here?"

"Actually," Callie began, inching out of the seat. "I think I'd prefer to just get takeout."

"It's fine." He glanced up at Kelly. "I'm leaving anyway."

"Callie?" Kelly questioned.

"Well, if Mr. Friendly here is leaving then I'm happy to stay." She eyed him across her glass of lemonade. His insouciance dug past her weariness and shock and provoked a hitherto slumbering source of bravery. "I'm sure he doesn't want to feel like any middle-aged women might dare to breathe in his general vicinity."

"I beg your pardon?"

Callie found a smile, aimed it at the waitress. "Apparently this gentleman thinks middle-aged women believe themselves to be entitled, which certainly sounds a little misogynistic to me."

"Is this true?" Kelly asked the man, hand on her hip, fire in her eyes.

"Look, I just call it as I see it. But hey, it's not surprising you're offended, seeing you're one of them too."

Regret kneaded Callie's heart at how she'd allowed the man's moment of ungraciousness to escalate in such a manner. But his unrepentant attitude shot new resolve within.

"Feel free to leave now," Kelly said, glaring at the man.

"Actually, you should pay first, shouldn't you?" Callie said, smiling sweetly at him.

"I don't want—" Kelly began.

"Oh, you do," murmured Callie, before saying in a louder voice, "because you wouldn't want Himbo here getting away with not paying simply because he insults those around him, would you? That would be the same as stealing, wouldn't it?"

The man—perhaps aware that nearby diners were turning to stare—seemed to lose his bluster and fished out his credit card and handed it to Kelly. He stood and moved to follow Kelly when the tanned beach-bum at the nearby table pushed his seat back, directly into his path. "Sorry, Barney."

The man muttered something she couldn't quite hear, the shaggy blond guy shrugged, and the unpleasant diner moved to the counter, where another exchange was followed by the man's snatch at his card and hasty escape.

Callie exhaled, tension leaving her chest, and glanced around. The older couple seated at the table and their surfer guest had returned to their conversation. All eyes were off her, and she could concentrate on her drink and on calming down. She pulled her hair from its usual low bun, letting it swing forward to hide her hot cheeks. Seriously. She would've been better off eating brown rice and wilted salad leaves at home.

Kelly came up with her food and placed it on the table. "I'm so sorry. That man was unbelievably rude."

"I should've just been happy with takeout," Callie said. "I really didn't mean to cause a scene."

"I, for one, am glad you did. I would've been happy to just have him leave, but at least with his credit card details we can ensure he doesn't visit here again. I don't want to see him, and I'm sure Granny Mae won't want his kind in here again."

Callie smiled, satisfaction streaming across her chest.

"That was your idea, wasn't it?" Kelly breathed.

"I hoped," she admitted.

"You're so smart."

"Maybe that's one perk of being middle-aged," Callie said wryly.

"Oh, honey. You're young still."

But being young *still* was a different matter to being young, wasn't it?

"I've got to admit that I didn't think thirty-three was quite at that age group, but maybe I'm just blessed with looking older than my age."

Kelly chuckled. "That might've been handy when you were younger and trying to get into bars."

"Bars have never really been my scene. Thank you for your help, and for this," she said, gesturing to her Caesar salad. "This looks delicious."

"It is, and it's on the house."

"Oh, but—"

"Don't argue. Granny Mae and I are both glad to have help to weed out the clientele we don't want."

"Well, thank you."

Callie's smile soon faded as the man's words came to mind again. Talk about entitled. Younger people never appreciated that they too would be this age one day. She propped her head in her hands, plunging her fork into the wide white bowl of salad, barely noticing what she ate. It was delicious and it filled her up, but whether it was lettuce, bacon, or crouton she didn't care.

Another glance around showed the place was starting to empty, as families and couples—no other singles here—went home. Went home to houses of their own, families of their own, children of their own.

Her eyes blurred, and she blinked away moisture. Seriously? Had the rude diner's words affected her so much? What chink in her armor had permitted his arrow to strike home? She was tougher than this. She always trusted God more than this. He had her future sorted, she knew. So why did she suddenly feel so old and pale and uninteresting, like the life she'd been granted wasn't enough? She was good at her job, she had friends, she had family, and she wasn't lonely.

Except now she rather felt that she was.

Made in the USA
Monee, IL
05 December 2021